GW00545120

30130 133139781

STRANGE INHERITANCE

STRANGE INHERITANCE

Serena Fairfax

CHIVERS
THORNDIKE

This Large Print edition is published by BBC Audiobooks Ltd, Bath, England and by Thorndike Press, Waterville, Maine, USA.

Published in 2004 in the U.K. by arrangement with the author.

Published in 2004 in the U.S. by arrangement with Dorian Literary Agency.

U.K. Hardcover   ISBN 0–7540–7691–1 (Chivers Large Print)
U.S. Softcover   ISBN 0–7862–5983–3 (General)

The text of this Large Print edition is unabridged.
Other aspects of the book may vary from the original edition.

Set in 16 pt. New Times Roman.

Printed in Great Britain on acid-free paper.

British Library Cataloguing in Publication Data available

Library of Congress Control Number: 2003111943

ESSEX COUNTY COUNCIL
LIBRARIES

CHAPTER ONE

Gemma's slim frame hunched tensely over her Honda motorbike as it jolted through the stormy January night. Behind her visor her sapphire-blue eyes dilated involuntarily as lightning streaked across the sky to light up the signpost—Fenwick 4 miles. Her stomach tightened with trepidation as she swung onto the narrow loop road. The bike's wheels hissed along its wet surface; a flurry of hailstones bounced off the crash helmet which hid her flame-coloured curls. Would this storm also bring disaster? The two had been inextricably linked for her since the age of eighteen, seven years ago. That time the storm had brought death to both her parents when their small rowing-boat capsized on Windermere. Then the devastation of loss had been softened by her Uncle Arthur's surprisingly kindly support. No-one would have guessed that a crusty bachelor, founder of a salmon canning business empire would have been capable of such unobtrusive help. But now there might be nothing to temper her sickening anticipation of its happening again. Uncle Arthur was fighting for his life in the intensive care unit of the infirmary. She accelerated and let it rip. It was a race against time—mercifully masking the all too cruel thought that she could be left

1

on her own.

Gemma flinched inwardly as the trees creaked ominously in the wind—her black-gloved hands instinctively hardening their grip on the handlebars. She checked the wing mirror and frowned. It was odd how much the car speeding behind resembled the Volvo Estate she'd seen parked in the lay-by at the crossroads. Her teeth began to chatter under her drenched black-leather biking jacket and damp had seeped through her tee-shirt to her very bones. Suddenly she registered the intermittent on-off, on-off flashing of the car's white headlights. It thoroughly unnerved her and she wondered how long it had been going on.

'Drat you,' she muttered, 'even bikes have a right to be on the road in this weather.'

She slowed down, and it followed suit to cruise silently, menacingly behind her signalling impatiently with its naked beam as it had done for more than half a mile.

'I should have stuck to the main road,' she scolded herself. It had been a crazy idea to make a detour via Fenwick where she'd planned to call the infirmary—which was in the same county, Northumberland—from the pub. But the present situation called for action not empty regrets. She glanced swiftly over her shoulder. That car was too close for comfort—she decided to change her tactics, watching with a certain satisfaction as the speedometer

2

needle momentarily shot past the speed limit.

But the car's big body thrust effortlessly forward to keep apace, the hard glare of its lights reflected in the wing mirrors dazzling her. She drew a sharp, terrified breath. Her forehead felt damp with sweat behind her visor. The car's horn hooted repeatedly. Its lights blazed—'like searchlights' Gemma thought, 'but I'm not a convict on the run.' She adjusted the angle of the screen and lowered her head; another wild gust of wind tore across her as she struggled to keep the Honda on course. The Volvo bore down on her and, pinned by its headlights, she slammed on the brakes. The bike squealed to a halt only inches from the ditch.

'What are you playing at?' The harshness in the man's deep voice fuelled her sense of alarm. A flash of lightning outlined the duffle-coated figure. Legs astride, hands on hips, the hood thrown back, he towered over her five feet six inches by six or seven inches, his lean face challenging.

Gemma said nothing, her heart pounding. She swung a leg over but stayed by the bike, her fears growing. Something in his hand moved and she recoiled instinctively but, as he pointed the object towards her, she saw it was not a cosh but a heavy, rubber-ended torch, and for a moment she was bathed in a small noose of light.

'I've been trying to get you to stop for the

3

last two miles but you've been riding like a maniac. There's an oak tree down, just before you reach the pub. The warning came over the car radio—I heard it just as you turned off. I had to let you know otherwise you'd have gone slap into it. You won't be able to get any further along here tonight. Dump your bike in the back and I'll run you over to the far end of Fenwick via the main road. Come on—you can't stay here all night.' There was a note of authority in the cultured voice.

'But I don't have to go along with it,' Gemma told herself. Her mouth felt suddenly dry. She folded her arms tightly across her chest, her usual ineffectual gesture of self-protection. She was almost sick with panic. She hadn't bargained for this. The man saw her hesitate.

'Are you daft, lad?' he asked curtly, 'what are you waiting for?'

He sounded as if he was accustomed to giving orders and having them obeyed, Gemma thought wryly.

'Get in now, there's plenty of room—for the two of you.' His tone was assured and faintly mocking as if he thought the rider was loath to leave a much-loved friend.

'Hurry up, look sharp, lad or . . .' the rest of his sentence was shredded by the sound of a tree crashing to the ground.

Gemma took one look at his face and that decided her. He seemed quite capable of

4

swooping down on her and bundling her bodily, bike and all into his Volvo. Reluctantly, she began to wheel the Honda round to the rear of the car and he raised the hatchback. He stood aside and jangled his keys watching her with ill-concealed impatience as she struggled to lift the bike into the back of it. It was on the tip of her tongue to ask him to give her a hand but she stopped herself in time. It was obvious he had mistaken her for a youth and, in the circumstances, it might be to her advantage to keep it that way. She stopped to catch her breath. The bike hadn't budged at all, its wheels still obstinately planted on the road.

'Like this, mate.' He grabbed hold of it and manhandled it in, slamming down the tailgate as she climbed in beside it. 'Just keep it upright.'

He reversed swiftly, going back the way they'd come. The main road glistened oily; whipped up by the wind the rain fell in a frenzied torrent, cancelling out the effect of the high-speed wipers. He made no attempt at small talk not even out of a sense of politeness, Gemma observed. From her crouching angle she could see the back of his arresting, dark head; his hair beginning to dry in the heated car curled slightly into the neck, and for one crazy moment she imagined her fingers threading through that thick, black hair which expensive cutting had not managed to tame.

5

He swore under his breath.

'It's quite impossible to carry on in these conditions—visibility's nil. I wonder if . . .?' He pulled off to the right onto a rough track, bumping along muddy ground until they came to a rickety farm gate. He got out to open it, leaving the engine idling.

'Now's my chance,' Gemma urged herself. She could make a dash for it. But almost immediately she realised it was hopeless. Without the bike, she was marooned—she wouldn't get far—and she couldn't heave that out single-handed. She groaned inwardly. The man returned to the car, and cautiously edged it forward; its tyres made slurping sounds as they wallowed across the water-logged field. They had only covered a short distance when he stopped again.

'Can't make it all the way. It's bound to get stuck.' He strode round to the back and beckoned, 'You'll have to get out now, I'm afraid.'

She had no alternative Gemma realised, her heart racing. Reluctantly she began to decant herself and as she collapsed towards him, he pulled her up quickly. Another gust of wind almost blasted her sideways and she stifled the instinctive cry for help which formed on her lips. He was already striding ahead expecting her to follow him. Gemma forced herself forward stumbling over debris-strewn farmland after him.

'Where are you taking me?' she once nearly called out.

'Not long now,' he shouted over his shoulder as if he had read her thoughts. He paused for a moment, a line between his brows as he watched her panting towards him.

'I'm done for,' Gemma thought dejectedly to herself. How was she going to get herself out of this? Despair began to prick at the back of her eyelids and she raised her visor slightly to dash away a tear. In her soggy trainers, her feet felt like blocks of ice. She and the man must have been squelching along for at least a quarter of an hour she reckoned, as she caught up with him.

'Over there—see it?' A small, stone barn loomed up out of the darkness. He stopped abruptly and she veered towards him.

'Hold it.' Long fingers briefly gripped her elbow, catching and steadying her, making her nerve ends tingle. He preceded her into the barn and shone his torch around and it picked up the shapes of rusting farm equipment.

'Well this isn't exactly virgin territory,' he said with a short laugh as he prowled around. Black graffiti and crudely sketched hearts and arrows scrawled with the words 'Wayne loves Tracey' completely covered one wall.

He left on the torch propping it up on a narrow shelf, and the gloom separated into eerie grey shapes. In the shadowy half-light, Gemma thought he looked foreign—rather

7

patrician with those high cheekbones in the tanned face. The straight, arrogant nose and the set of the jaw and mouth hinted at an individuality quite different from conventional male good looks. At a guess he seemed about ten to twelve years older than she was.

He lowered himself to the floor, leaning his supple body against the wall. He stretched out his long legs and kicked off his thick, rubber boots. Totally absorbed in what he was doing, he began to peel off his red socks, his feet surprisingly slender for a man of his height. What other clothes was he going to remove? Panic clutched at Gemma and she looked away uneasily, shifting into a circle of light. He glanced up as he wrung out his socks.

'Training to be an astronaut, lad?' He jerked a thumb at her crash helmet, his lips curving in amusement. The moment she had been dreading had arrived. Gemma slowly removed her gloves and undid the chin-band with trembling fingers. She lifted off the crash helmet and the glossy red hair tumbled to her shoulders.

'So! Benedict is Beatrice.' He said it swiftly, fiercely—an undertone of anger in his surprise at her deliberate ploy to mislead him. He rose to his feet and gave a deep, exaggerated bow. 'At your service, madam.' Ocean-green eyes travelled over her in a sharp, slow appraisal, registering the creamy skin with its delicate colouring, the *retroussé* nose, the soft inviting lips that were invariably curved in a smile now pursed. She looked at him warily under level brows, the 'road lid' cradled under her arm, unaware of the expressions which flitted across her face. Doubt, anguish, fear—he could read them all.

'And your bike's the same colour as your eyes.' Humour lurked in the sensuous line of his mouth. The observation was totally unexpected but she met his gaze.

'Art not design,' she managed weakly.

'And if I'm not mistaken, eye shadow to match.'

There was no answer to that one, Gemma thought ruefully, particularly as she was sure it had begun to run. She dabbed at it ineffectively.

He unbuttoned his duffle-coat and threw it down on the cold, rough floor and flung himself down on it.

'This makes a passable rug.' He patted it and she hesitated.

'Come on now, lass, you can't possibly stand there all night.'

He was right, of course, she thought dismally as she gingerly eased herself onto it. She drew up her knees, trying to keep as much distance as she could between herself and that lean, powerful body. Sitting or standing, she was no match for his tempered steel.

Suddenly, uncontrollably, she began to sneeze. She groped for a handkerchief.

9

'You'll need more than that.' He ripped off his navy Guernsey pullover, revealing a maroon shirt. 'Put this on.' He pushed the pullover across. 'You'll catch your death if you don't get those wet things off.'

Thick and heavy, it was tempting; Gemma was torn between a desire for comfort and an instinct for self-preservation. He shot her a quizzical glance and laughed, a rich, deep sound.

'Your look speaks volumes. I promise not to look—not even a sly peek—nor will I lay siege to that remarkable armour plating.' He shut his eyes with an exaggerated snap that somehow heightened the tension that knotted her stomach.

She turned her back on him, two scarlet spots of colour high on her cheekbones, removing everything but her panties and rolled up her sodden garments into a small bundle. She pulled his sweater over her head; it was still warm from his body heat and smelled faintly of talc. She glanced down at it. It was very long—reaching almost to her knees—and too large, the chest hanging round her like a piece of sacking. The sleeves dangled well below her wrists and she hitched them up to her elbows.

His mouth curved in a smile. 'You could sell that as the latest in fashionably distressed women's wear.' Under his open-necked shirt, she could see dark chest hair below the

10

powerful shaft of his neck. It was strangely disturbing.

'So you think I'm distressed?' she bantered lightly. She shifted slightly on the duffle and the soft material of his shirt brushed against her breasts. She drew hurriedly away, her nerve ends raw.

'Look, you're quite safe with me, if that's what's worrying you.' His eyes were veiled.

'That wasn't on my mind,' she returned icily, but she read the scepticism in his face. Her initial relief gave way to apprehension. That was what he'd be bound to say. Allay her fears only to strike later. Well she wouldn't let her guard down.

'And as we've been thrown together we must try and make the best of it.' He continued pointedly, 'What possessed you to expose yourself on a night like this?' He flung the challenge at her, amusement flaring up in his face.

He was master of the situation and of her, Gemma realised, but she refused to be needled.

'It was fine when I started out,' she began calmly. 'Then the works manager rang me at Uncle's home—you see I was spending a long weekend with him up here—to tell me they'd rushed him from the factory to the hospital by ambulance and I . . .' she faltered. Her worries about Uncle Arthur flooded back with a new, painful intensity.

11

'Go on,' he encouraged gently. His gaze was searching.

'I should have arrived there hours ago—but this freak weather blew up . . . oh God . . .' her voice tailed off.

He caught the anguish in her tone, 'A storm like this will soon blow itself out. I'm sure your uncle's getting the best possible care. You've got to believe that,' he said kindly, touching her arm sympathetically.

'I'll try,' she said sombrely, not daring to think otherwise.

Draughts of cold air blew through the gap beneath the badly fitting barn door and Gemma jumped at a new volley of thunder.

'Well this is a story I'll be dining out on in years to come,' she forced a light note into her voice.

'Ah! Do I detect a giddy social life?' He probed the oval of her face. He might just as well have come out with it—'Are you attached—what about the man in your life?'

'Does work leave much time for that?' she countered refusing to be drawn, conscious that she'd revealed much more than she'd intended to this stranger about whom she had learned absolutely nothing.

He laughed throwing back his head to show even, white teeth. 'Don't you know? The more you do, the more time you can find to do it in.' He had shut his eyes and when he opened them, they danced wickedly.

'Well, I dare say it applies to you,' Gemma observed stiffly, trying to weigh up this man who knew so well how to use those green eyes. Cultured and obviously monied—if the Volvo was anything to go by. Probably an efficient manager of his time—the same could not be said of her, she thought wryly.

'That's an extraordinary assumption,' he smiled broadly and bent his head so that his warm body was only inches from her. Gemma registered the pull of his raw masculinity. He was utterly attractive—experienced, no doubt, and very, very dangerous. An electric shiver ran through her and she sat rigidly upright, trying to ignore his nearness—but it was impossible. She knew now with total conviction that for her own protection she had to avoid any more actual physical contact with him. Then she began to reproach herself. How on earth could she feel like this about a man she had only just met and certainly did not know—was not even sure that she liked?

'Tell me how you figured that out,' he pressed, his voice oddly seductive.

Gemma shrugged and deliberately moved slightly, shattering the intimacy which floated between them.

'Pure guesswork,' her hands trembled a little as she pushed back an errant strand of hair. 'But am I right?' she demanded suddenly, staring back defiantly.

'That's not for me to say,' he said lightly,

13

'but do go on—I'm riveted to hear your analysis of me—quite irresistible—and very provocative.'

Her face flamed and Gemma dropped her eyes to the makeshift rug. He was not only dangerous but very clever, adroitly deflecting her questions. It was a skill honed by constant practice.

'I didn't mean it to sound like that,' she said tautly, 'I was simply . . .'

'. . . trying to place me?' he asked lazily but the green eyes were intent.

Gemma moistened her lips. What on earth had possessed her to start out on this tack?

'Never mind.' She was aware of his warm smile. But she noticed that he still didn't volunteer anything about himself.

'How do you enjoy being a public sector employee?' he asked conversationally.

'What makes you think . . . how do you know?' Gemma's head went up quickly and her eyes widened with surprise.

'Easy,' he jerked a thumb at her rolled-up jacket, 'that sticker on the sleeve—"better books at your local library".'

He misses nothing, Gemma thought.

'I designed it,' Gemma found herself telling him, explaining she was a community librarian with a South London borough.

'Is that some sort of buzz word?' His eyes went over her in a way that made her feel oddly breathless. He delved into a pocket and

14

withdrew a bar of chocolate, breaking it in half.

'You make it sound like a non job,' Gemma grumbled.

'Is it?' he teased.

'You're impossible,' she stormed and launched into a defence of her work. Her father had been an historian and it was a natural progression for her to work in a local museum. 'We show how yesterday provided the foundations for today. Our displays are about how the locality once was, what it's like now, and the stages by which it changed into the layout we have today. Like those blocks of flats were once grand Victorian houses and the school was built on the site of an old country mansion surrounded by acres of woodland. The nineteenth-century slums have been pulled down and replaced by hypermarkets.'

She paused to nibble the chocolate, suddenly conscious of gnawing hunger pangs.

'And what about different life-styles and the cost of living. Wouldn't those comparisons be relevant?' His relaxed air belied the fact that he listened intently. Gemma continued enthusiastically, her love of her job manifestly genuine. 'Oh, we've got every little thing we can lay our hands on—the price of a bar of soap, fifty years ago and what it cost to have a wedding then—you'd *never* believe the difference. It's a community museum because a lot of the objects were given to us by local people. We cover a wide range of things past and present showing tradition and change—like sport, transport, work, home. We also mount special exhibitions about the way of life of our ethnic neighbours. I love it—it's very interesting,' she added softly.

When she finished she noticed that he was watching her under lowered lids, his arms folded across his chest.

'When you're excited, your eyes shine.'

Her colour heightened and taken aback she had no ready answer to that.

*   *   *

She felt furious at herself for having fallen into the trap he'd laid to talk about herself. Abruptly she got to her feet and walked barefoot to the barn entrance, looking out into the storm-tossed night. It was bitterly cold. She felt almost numb . . . She moved away from the door, the ceiling began to waver—her knees felt like water. She reached up an arm against the wall to steady herself. Immediately he was beside her, an arm about her shoulders holding her to his solid, warm body.

'Are you all right?' There was a note of genuine concern in his voice.

She swallowed hard, 'I don't know what came over me.' Her legs still felt wobbly. He continued to support her, a line between his brows, his eyes searching her face. The break in her voice wasn't lost on him.

'Come on—you're exhausted. Try and get some sleep—it's going to be a long night,' he said gently.

Gemma pulled away a little, her heart thudding unevenly and dropped to her spot on the duffle, her knees drawn up to her chin, trying to maintain her distance from him, which was not so very distant in the small space which separated them. She couldn't allow herself to sleep—not with him so close to her, but she didn't relish spending the night fighting him off. Each time she felt herself drifting into slumber, she jerked herself awake. He seemed to be wide awake regarding her thoughtfully. She could smell the storm and hear it and once it seemed as if it might rip up the barn and hurl it about.

Once tossed out of an uneasy sleep by a flash of forked lightning, Gemma found her head buried on his chest, her limbs close up against that hard, lean body, his breath warm against her temple. She drew away, her lips grazing his cheek. A gentle, amused smile touched the corners of his mouth as his eyes lowered to her mouth.

Again, feeling cold she woke and looked into his sleeping features. Even in repose, the lean, boned face was strong and the urge to trail her fingers through his hair was almost uncontrollable. How she wished the night was over. Half waking, half sleeping, she was

17

terrified lest he take her unawares. She moved, trying to find a more comfortable position and he stirred in his sleep. But by now she began to feel decidedly drowsy again. She sank down into the gloom, her eyelids heavy.

Gemma woke to a thin pencil of light under the door. There was no sign of the man, and she felt a faint flutter of panic. She was completely alone and he had gone—but wasn't that what she'd wanted—to be left alone? She huddled on the floor, close to tears. She looked down at his sweater and then remembered her own clothing. It would be dry by now, she thought. She felt the colour rush to her cheeks as she saw them neatly spread out, hanging from the dilapidated bits of farm machinery in the corner of the barn. While she slept, he had sorted out the sodden bundle and hung them to dry. She fingered them. Her bra and tee-shirt were dry, and the leather jacket was no worse for the deluge but the jeans were still damp, although the worst had been wrung out and they could be worn again for the short journey ahead.

She grimaced at herself in the mirror of her compact.

'What a fright I look,' she thought. Tangled curls, make up non-existent; her face felt quite naked without it—smudged eye shadow. 'God what a mess,' she muttered irritably. She shut it with a snap.

Suddenly the door burst open, the morning

light almost blinding her.

'Awake at last—sleep well?' He stood at the door, his eyes on her flushed cheeks. He looked as if he'd been up for some time and, despite the five o'clock shadow, he looked fresh and rested, his eyes very bright. 'You slept like a log.' There was a glint of mischief in his gaze.

'It may have seemed like that to you,' she fought to keep her voice cool. Now that he was still here, perversely she wanted him gone. 'I slept after a fashion.' He tilted his head, his green eyes sweeping her critically,

'You slept the sleep of the just.'

He was infuriating Gemma thought but with a bit of luck this would be the last she'd see of him. The thought threaded a strange feeling of bitter-sweet through her and she pushed past him stepping into the morning.

'You see—it's a jewel of a day.'

'I can see that,' she tossed back caustically. He was devastatingly handsome even in the cold light of day and for some reason that irritated her. She felt in a strange mood this morning as if last night's storm had tossed her about like a sapling leaving her with a set of conflicting emotions.

'Sleep hasn't improved your temper,' he drawled. Gemma didn't answer for a moment. She stepped outside, gulping draughts of cold, icy air—it was almost intoxicating. The fresh smell of damp country soil rose from the ground.

'Nor has it altered your ability to rile me,' she returned, ducking back into the barn under his arm, his thigh brushing the curve of her hip. She thought she saw a momentary flash of impatience in the emerald eyes.

'Rile you?' he repeated raising a quizzical brow. He watched her like a lynx, following her every move as she looped her 'road lid' over her wrist. 'After you've been so open with me—why should I want to do that?'

Something in his tone made her freeze. Her blue eyes widened. She didn't like the way he said that. She rummaged in her bag and dragged a comb ferociously through the tumbled disarray of her hair. Her thoughts raced ahead as she tried to piece together the sequence of the night's events. What exactly had happened? she wondered wildly. It seemed all very blurred now in the cold light of day—like a rapidly fading dream. All she could remember was nodding off and waking up to find her breasts yielding to the hardness of his chest.

'Can you be more specific?' Gemma asked huskily. She had to know—did she let him make love to her in return for his protection? The thought of intimacy with this man—this stranger—made her body respond in a way she fought to disguise. Awareness of him as a man was what she wanted least at this moment. She darted him a furious look.

20

'Oh I don't think we've got time to spend on the small print.' His mouth quirked. But there was something else in his steady gaze that made her feel as if he had stripped her bare. She drew a deep, long breath—she could see he was not going to let her pursue it. And where was her sense of proportion? she asked herself. He was being maddeningly evasive so she probably hadn't compromised herself and anyway, it was not something she would easily have forgotten. Or would she? The memory had an amazing capacity to blank out the inconvenient. Doubt nagged at the back of her mind.

She held out his pullover, 'Thanks for the loan,' she said awkwardly.

'Do keep it, you'll need it,' he said and stooped to retrieve his duffle-coat. He shrugged it on and gave a brief, swift look round the barn, before stepping outside again.

'But I don't want to.' Gemma was equally determined, quickening her pace to keep up with his long stride as he headed back to the abandoned Volvo. She didn't want it. She didn't want anything that would remind her that she had slipped out of emotional control, and allowed him to invade her private space. There was a short, tense pause.

'Then give it to Oxfam,' he flung over his shoulder.

'No,' Gemma said breathlessly, as she caught him up. 'You can do that.' Why was her heart racing like this? Was it because she'd almost been running or that he was only inches away?

He stopped abruptly and turned to face her, the set of his jaw suggesting controlled annoyance.

'You seem to have a sort of death wish—first a close shave with a mighty oak and now you're courting pneumonia. Surely your life has something good going for it?'

Gemma gasped, feeling stunned. Their eyes clashed. She wasn't going to let him get away with that sort of remark.

'How dare you,' she seethed, unaware of her clenched fists, her fingernails biting deep into the flesh of her palm, 'That's bloody unfair,' she exploded. 'I . . .'

'Look, just keep the pullover and your outraged feelings for some other time. I've a meeting to get to.' His sudden burst of irritation was replaced by ice but it was no less alarming.

'And am I supposed to be detaining you?' Gemma questioned silently.

'Well don't let me keep you,' she managed sarcastically.

'Don't worry—you're not,' he got in the last word, hooking his thumbs into the waistband of his trousers. He gave her a brief half smile.

An odd unwarranted sense of rebuff swelled up in her and she strove to suppress it, worrying her lower lip with her teeth.

They reached the spot where he'd left his car the previous night and effortlessly he removed her bike for her, placing it carefully on the ground.

Gemma depressed the kick-start lever, strands of hair falling across her face, semi-masking it. The engine stubbornly refused to turn.

'Damn,' she muttered under her breath, and tried again, flurried.

'It's probably cold,' he observed, his body tantalisingly close to hers.

Gemma didn't reply, pushing back the curtain of hair, exasperated. Why did he have to state the obvious in that infuriating manner? She kick-started again but there was no answering roar from the engine. The bike had never let her down before—it mustn't now, she prayed.

'Plenty of petrol in it?' There was humour in his eyes.

She bit back the retort that sprang to her lips.

'Of course,' she said starchily. There was nothing he could teach her about motorcycles. The thought of her superior know-how cheered her up and she applied another kick start with renewed vigour.

'Let me have a look at it.' He took command. Gemma moved aside. Well if he wanted to advertise his ignorance . . . she thought gleefully.

He bent over the machine, his long, broad back towards her. There was a quick flick of his wrist.

'Right—now have another go.'

Gemma sniffed unconvinced, 'Can't see where that'll get me.'

'To your destination.' He laid a hand on her shoulder.

She shrugged sceptically and twisted away out of his reach, her stomach fluttering. Resignedly she tried again and the engine fired richly.

'How on earth . . .' Gemma gawped at him, her eyes round.

'Easy,' he grinned, without a trace of modesty. 'The ignition switch was in the "off" position. You must have caught it accidentally with your sleeve. It's much easier than you imagine to do something like that.'

Gemma adjusted the crash helmet over her hair, furious with herself, and gave him a murmured thanks, colour burning her cheeks. She settled herself in the saddle and tilted her head towards him surveying him from behind the anonymity of the visor, and met his eyes boldly.

'*Bonne chance.*' He stepped back and smiled broadly, a hand raised in salute.

Gemma had to return the smile. As she accelerated away, she felt his gaze boring into her back. Something inside her dissolved, split. She half looked back, floundering in an odd blend of relief and loss. She'd found it hard to believe when rescued hostages reported a certain bonding with their captors but now, after that enforced night of shelter in the isolated barn, she began to understand what they meant. The bike juddered beneath her in the fresh morning air as she rounded a corner. It was time to forget the events of the storm—less easy to forget the man she'd shared them with.

*   *   *

Mrs Moore patted her neat grey-haired bun. 'Well, if you're sure you'll be all right . . .' she said tentatively, looking suspiciously red-eyed.

Gemma touched her uncle's housekeeper gently on the arm.

'I'm positive—you've been wonderful. Now go off and have a lie down. It's been a very hectic day for you both.'

'Well now, if you insist, Miss Gemma. But mind, if there's anything you need—anything at all we can do, we're just up the road in the cottage. Oh dear, it won't be the same without Mr Wells.' She dabbed her eyes, her rather stern features softened by grief.

Gemma nodded, a lump in her throat.

'He was a right good employer—one of the best. It's only fitting that he should get a proper burial.' She twisted her wedding ring round and round on her finger.

'And I can't thank you enough. I'd never have managed all that catering single-handed.' Gemma's appreciation was heart felt.

The last of the mourners had left 'Four Winds', her uncle's house. Not until the funeral had Gemma realised the wealth of affection and regard in which Uncle Arthur was held. Solemn-faced businessmen pumped her hand sympathetically, their condolences full of genuine warmth.

'Good day then, Miss Gemma and to you, Mr Hanson.' Mrs Moore nodded mournfully at the man who had been Arthur Wells's solicitor for the last forty years. Mr Hanson clasped her hand in a firm grip, the eyes shrewd behind the half-moon spectacles. The housekeeper walked stiffly out of the large drawing-room as if she was carrying an enormous burden. Gemma heard the click of the back door and crossed to the front window watching silently as Mrs Moore and her husband shuffled past.

Gemma sighed, feeling utterly drained. 'They've been with uncle for as long as I can remember,' she remarked sadly.

'Indeed,' Mr Hanson was bald and whippet-thin. 'I well remember the day Arthur asked me to vet them. He wasted no time making up his mind once I'd given him the all-clear. The very next morning they were hard at it—scrubbing, cooking, gardening and chauffeuring. That must have been—let me see now, getting on for thirty years ago. But, of course, that was typical of Arthur. Once he made up his mind to do a thing, it was as good as done. Even during this last illness of his, he was a businessman to the end.' There was a note of admiring approval in his voice.

Gemma was only half listening, 'Both out of a job now,' her voice was tinged with regret. 'I can't possibly afford to keep them on.' Her mouth felt dry and she rose to her feet to fortify herself with brandy.

'Can I offer you anything?' she asked the solicitor. Her hands shook a little as cognac splashed from the crystal decanter into the glass.

'Later my dear, later.' He seemed to be preoccupied—twiddling the combination on his pig-skin brief-case and snapping it open.

He cleared his throat importantly and surveyed her silently for a few moments over the top of his spectacles. It was all very theatrical, Gemma thought morosely, cradling the balloon glass in her hands.

'No point in beating about the bush. Arthur would have wanted me to get on with it.'

'Get on with what?' Gemma asked, wearily wondering why Mr Hanson had lingered on well after the others had gone. Now, as he took out a buff, foolscap envelope from his case with a decided flourish, she knew.

'Can't it wait?' she protested feebly, emotionally exhausted by the events of the day. She leaned back on the plump, feather-filled cushions and laid the glass down on the polished rosewood side table.

Mr Hanson looked reproachful. 'Arthur,' he stressed heavily, 'never believed in procrastination—the thief of time,' he added unnecessarily.

'And time is something we do not have.' Gemma murmured her uncle's well-worn phrase under her breath.

'Do you think I could have your attention?' Mr Hanson said sharply, as though he thoroughly disapproved of her lack of interest in her uncle's Will. He took off his spectacles and polished them with unnecessary vigour, Gemma observed idly.

She smoothed down the front of her black woollen dress and crossed one black, sheeny stockinged leg over the other. A wintry afternoon sun shone through the windows, and lit up the collection of antique silver in the glass-fronted show case, making it gleam.

'First of all,' he slit open the envelope, 'let me allay your immediate concerns. The Moores are well provided for. They get to remain in the cottage on a generous pension.'

Gemma smiled delightedly. 'Thank heavens for that—how kind of uncle. I'm so relieved— Mr Moore loves the cottage garden. It would have been a terrible wrench for them if they'd had to vacate.' It was a load off her mind.

'Then there are some legacies to various

close friends—long-standing cronies. I think I'll change my mind, if I may.' He rose to his feet and poured himself a double measure of whisky. Gemma wondered if he was playing for time—trying to find the right words to soften the blow. She had no expectations. Why should she? Uncle had supported her generously during his life. There were probably more deserving relatives—distant cousins in Australia and Canada with whom she knew he ritually exchanged cards at Christmas and birthdays.

Mr Hanson took a sip of his whisky. 'The residue of his estate—and it is considerable, my dear, Arthur has bequeathed to you.'

For a moment it didn't register. 'Me? Are you quite sure?' Gemma gasped, and leaned forward amazed, her hands clasped round her knees.

Mr Hanson frowned and Gemma realised that in her incredulity she had said the wrong thing—it sounded as if she was impugning his professional skills.

'Of course, you must be—only it's just that I . . .' she ventured uncertainly, retreating into the solid comfort of the chair.

Mr Hanson's expression softened and his brown eyes snapped with the pleasure of being the bearer of good tidings.

'No need to be so surprised. Arthur was very fond of you.'

Gemma swallowed hard and sipped some

brandy, smoothing her hair back from her face. Fondness, affection—these were not things uncle wore on his sleeve. A gruff, feudal figure, she had no idea that she occupied such a special corner of his heart.

'There is, however, one more thing.' The solicitor's booming voice cut across her thoughts. 'Your fortune has been put in a trust fund which will only be released to you on certain specific conditions.'

Gemma's head jerked up sharply, her expression puzzled. 'I don't understand—isn't that rather unusual? After all, I am of age.'

There was a long, dense silence while Mr Hanson regarded her over the top of his whisky glass. Gemma stared back at him, her mind in a complete whirl. There was no logic in it—it was like giving with one hand, and taking with the other.

'Arthur wouldn't tell me why he wanted it that way and I did not press him. He was entitled to keep his reasons to himself,' he added pompously.

'What sort of conditions, then?' Gemma persisted uneasily. She had to know.

Mr Hanson's thin mouth turned down, 'Now there I can't help you. All I do know is that Arthur asked me to deliver a letter from him to your trustee which sets out the conditions precisely.' He sounded guarded.

'Trustee—what do you mean? Aren't you my trustee?' Gemma broke in anxiously, her face pale.

Mr Hanson shook his head and pretended to consult the Will again, 'Your trustee is Stefan Radulescu.'

Gemma's head reeled, 'What . . . Stefan Radu . . .' she tripped over the strange pronunciation. 'Is this a joke? May I?' She reached out a hand for the Will. It was typewritten on thick, white legal stationery and ran to just one page. Brevity was Uncle Arthur's hallmark. It gave her a jolt to see his signature at the bottom—in royal blue ink, it flowed boldly and as freshly as if it had been signed that day.

She read out aloud, 'I appoint Stefan Radulescu of Eaton Square, Belgravia, London to be the sole executor and trustee of this my Will.' Her voice trembled slightly.

'No joke, my dear. That wasn't Arthur's style at all. He had the highest regard for Stefan's integrity. Your trustee is well known to me as a brilliant barrister, indeed I have sought his counsel on several complex cases myself. What you might call a trouble-shooter.'

Gemma twisted the single chain of pearls round her throat, lustrous against the creamy column of her neck. 'It's intriguing.' It was all she could find to say. 'How did they come to know each other?' Uncle couldn't have met him in London—he professed to hate the capital and claimed to have visited it only once—reluctantly—during the last twenty-five years.

'Stefan owns several thousand acres in the county and that's how they met, I believe, through the local landowners' association,' Mr Hanson replied. Gemma subsided, her emotions jangling confusedly inside her. A substantial inheritance, but there was a catch to it. Mr Hanson who she knew and relied on had been relegated. This man with the foreign sounding name was tied in with her whether she liked it or not. She felt stranded between joy and dismay—lifted up one moment and hurled about in the next.

'Rather outlandish name,' Gemma said at last, rather tartly.

Mr Hanson chuckled, lightening the atmosphere, 'Well we British are a nation of foreigners. But I can see you want to know more about him—that's understandable.' His brown eyes registered her barely concealed curiosity. 'I have already written to tell him of Arthur's death but I'm told by his chambers that he's unavoidably abroad at present, otherwise he would have been here today at Arthur's funeral and you could have met him and got all this business over with. But he's certain to contact you on his return so don't fret. In the meantime, all I can say is that I don't think you'll find him unreasonable. Now . . .' he shuffled the papers in his case, 'here's a copy of Arthur's Will—go through it at your leisure and if there's anything you want me to clarify, just let me know.'

*   *   *

Gemma saw him to the door and waved until his blue Rolls Corniche was out of sight. He didn't seem unduly upset at being passed over as trustee—in fact, it seemed quite the reverse, she mused as she carefully rinsed the glasses under the tap. But then he had nothing to worry about. Stefan's whatshisname was bound to instruct him to apply for probate of the Will so he'd get his fancy fee in the end. So it was all the same to him, she supposed with a heavy sigh. She'd always suspected Mr Hanson was all for a simple life. Perhaps the terms of the trust were too arduous or he preferred not to get involved. She could almost hear his plummy voice smoothly agreeing with uncle over their weekly game of chess. 'Stefan will do admirably' thus ridding himself neatly of any jousting with aggrieved parties.

*   *   *

Gemma wandered back to the drawing-room and took up her copy of her uncle's Will. It was a complete mystery to her why he had set up the trust and she could find no clues in the document itself. She crossed to the window—a Volvo very similar to that owned by the man in the storm flashed by, full of laughing children.

33

She was instantly taken back to that night—was it only a week ago? Despite the worries of the last few days—the vigil by her uncle's bedside and now his funeral, the man's face remained as fresh in her mind as if the incident had occurred only yesterday. Why should she remember him, when she could scarcely remember the faces of some of the boys in her year at college—boys who she had seen day in and day out while they were all under-graduates?

The telephone jangled impatiently at her elbow. Gemma hesitated, trying to compose herself. Could this be Stefan?

She picked it up and there was the sound of a familiar trill. 'Pip!' Gemma called down the receiver. Her friend's voice was like a breath of fresh air after the gloom of the last few days, yet a strange feeling of disappointment invaded her.

*   *   *

'It all sounds pretty odd to me,' Pip remarked candidly after Gemma had explained about the trust. 'Hang on a minute—I'll just get this beef Wellington out of the oven.' Gemma could visualise her friend in her kitchen surrounded by the delicious concoctions she prepared as a free-lance cook. 'What's your next move.' She had returned to the telephone.

Gemma said slowly, 'I don't think its up to me. I'm certain Mr Hanson knows more than he's letting on, though. It just looks as if I'll have to contain myself until my trustee gets in touch first.'

'Old Hanson's a crafty devil.' Pip's summing up was uncannily accurate. 'Still I don't suppose this Stefan chap will keep you on tenterhooks for long. After all, he'll want to get the administration of your uncle's estate under way.'

'Hmmm—you're probably right.' Gemma was far from convinced but it was simpler to agree with Pip. She felt in her bones there was a time bomb ticking away. 'Anyway, there's no point my staying up here any longer—it's kind of creepy on my own, rattling away in this huge place like a pea in a pod. I'd much rather be at home.'

'But "Four Winds" is your second home now, isn't it?' Pip asked bluntly.

Gemma gave a short laugh, 'Not until my trustee's signed it over to me—if and when—that is. Anyway, I've decided to lock up here and head back tomorrow.'

'You sound pretty fed up.' Pip sounded concerned. 'Are you sure you don't want me up there to keep you company?'

'No.' The rebuff was swift, uncharacteristic. In her vulnerable state, Gemma was sure Pip would whittle out of her the events of the storm and, for some reason which defied

35

analysis, she didn't want to talk about it.

'Oh.' Pip digested the sharp retort. Gemma was obviously very cut up—it wasn't like her to be so dismissive. Then she spoke again, an urgent note in her voice. 'Got it. Radulescu— the surname's Romanian. Like that famous playwright, Eugene Ionescu—the ending's the same. Shades of Dracula,' she gave a smothered laugh, 'sounds as if he's found his true vocation as your trustee. There'll be a fair amount of blood letting there.'

'Don't,' begged Gemma, struggling with a sudden surge of alarm. Her mental picture of Stefan as a desiccated, humourless lawyer was bad enough without Pip's ghoulish embellishments. 'Why, oh why, Uncle,' she thought for the umpteenth time, 'couldn't you have made things simpler?'

'Okay—I'll get in some stores for you,' Pip's ever practical mind raced ahead.

Next morning, Gemma did a swift check of the large, grey stone house, making sure the doors and windows were properly secured. She scribbled a hasty note to Mrs Moore, reminding her where she could be found in an emergency. Not that she expected the place to burn down . . .

The heavy oak door thudded behind her. It was one of those rare January mornings when the sun shone brightly from a clear, blue sky and the air was invigoratingly cold. Back home, the routine of work was like an

36

anaesthetic, blotting out the pain of bereavement and the perplexing nature of the bequest.

*   *   *

'Any news yet?' Pip sank her teeth into a large cream doughnut in the coffee shop of the large West End department store where the winter sales were in full swing. Gemma needed new curtains for her flat but had decided to wait until the expensive material which she had yearned after was marked down to an affordable price. It was an economy of which Uncle Arthur would have approved. And she would run them up herself on Pip's high-tec Japanese electronic sewing-machine.

Gemma swallowed hurriedly, hot coffee scalding the back of her throat. 'Not a thing— not a squeak. I do hope this won't clash with the carpet' she muttered worriedly, peering into the carrier bag again. Doubtfully she fingered the heavy glazed material with its bold slashes of contrasting colour— appropriately called 'Mondrian'.

'I've told you it's a perfect match. But that's not what's bugging you?' she eyed her friend shrewdly, her hazel eyes thoughtful.

Gemma tapped the spoon against the side of the cup and it gave out the dull sound of metal against pottery.

'No . . . you're right. I wish my trustee would

37

get things moving. I have this niggling feeling that it's not going to be plain sailing. And I hate being in a state of suspended animation.' Her voice rose with agitation. That morning she had discovered the Guernsey sweater in her pillion bag and the night with the stranger flooded back—fresh, unforgettable. She'd pressed the sweater to her cheek and it still carried that faint, yet unmistakable smell of him.

Pip said nothing, knowing all too well how Gemma felt. Ever since they'd first met at a motor bike scramble six years ago, she'd realised that patience was not one of Gemma's strong points. But this was different. She'd never seen her so jumpy.

'Have you thought of taking the bull by the horns—contacting him off your own bat?' she asked tentatively as she demolished the remains of the doughnut. That put paid to her New Year's resolution to go on a strict diet.

Gemma rubbed the tip of her nose and gave a wide, unexpected smile. 'It had crossed my mind.'

Pip grinned broadly at the understatement.

'But I invariably end up telling myself to wait and see what happens, even though I'm like a cat on hot bricks.'

'Didn't Mr Hanson say Stefan was away on business?' Pip reminded her, clutching at straws. 'That's probably delayed things.' Privately she thought Stefan was a swine for

38

keeping Gemma in a vacuum.

'That was weeks ago,' Gemma exploded suddenly, her face a blaze of anger. She toyed with a piece of apple strudel, 'Actually, I rang Mr Hanson on some pretext yesterday and he was genuinely surprised I'd heard nothing more.'

'Had he received any feedback at all from Stefan?' Pip enquired, 'It might give us something to go on.'

'Just an acknowledgement,' Gemma sounded mournful. 'Routine sort of letter, I gathered. Sorry to hear about Uncle's death etcetera—you know the usual stuff and saying he'd commence his duties as trustee shortly. It all sounded very formal and pompous.'

Pip laid down her cup suddenly so that it clattered on the saucer, 'I've got it,' she said excitedly, just give him until the end of next week. Then, if he still hasn't made a move, you do it—just pick up the phone . . . !'

Gemma groaned and covered her eyes with a hand, 'I couldn't Pip, honestly. I know I'm no shrinking violet but this is . . . different.'

'. . . or drop him a line,' she swept on, 'hand deliver it,' she suggested with an extravagant sweep of her hand.

Gemma began to giggle.

Pip warmed to her theme, 'What about a balloon over Eaton Square—come in Stefan, your number is up? That'll galvanise him into action. Or what about a . . . strippagram?'

Gemma rocked with laughter at Pip's outrageous ideas. Her eyes filled with water, tension easing from her. Pip made it sound so easy, but she knew that in this particular case she wouldn't have the nerve to initiate anything.

Pip glanced at her watch and reluctantly pushed back her chair, 'Richard is throwing a party tonight and typically has persuaded me to do the cooking for him. I haven't been able to wriggle out of it, so duty calls.'

Richard was her twin brother, a trainee accountant, with whom she unwillingly shared a shabby, rambling flat. Gemma waggled an admonishing finger at her friend. 'Now who's letting herself be pushed around?' she teased.

They made for their motorbikes.

'This isn't the same thing,' Pip retorted with a grin, as she halted her Suzuki outside the gloomy mansion block where she lived.

*   *   *

She was right, thought Gemma as she sped away. She couldn't continue waiting for Stefan—the inertia was paralysing. If she hadn't heard from him by tomorrow . . . no, say, this time next week, she'd ginger him up herself. The thought made her feel light-hearted. Soon uncle's secret would be revealed—for better or for worse.

40

CHAPTER TWO

Gemma took a long, deep breath of expectation and wondered what lay in store for her. She stepped through the narrow archway that led from the noise and bustle of Fleet Street and it was as if she had entered another world, the cacophony of everyday sounds miraculously excluded. She had left her bike at home that day and now she picked her way carefully along the unevenly paved path that ran by King's Bench Walk. This was The Temple which had housed barristers' quarters from the Middle Ages. Beyond an old stone fountain, well-manicured lawns rolled down to the Embankment.

The summons, to which she likened Stefan's letter when it arrived that morning, was incisive. The black squiggle on the formal writing-paper was indecipherable, but his name was printed beneath it in bold type. A clock chimed four o'clock as she mounted the stone steps to his chambers. He had not offered an alternative date or time; Gemma's increasing sense of anticipation had given way to exasperation at the man who she felt had dangled her along until early February and then suddenly asked her to attend to his convenience. She'd been half inclined to refuse—to tell him that in her world—the 'real' world, these things took time to arrange. She couldn't just bury her obligations at the drop of a hat. But there was something in the tone of his letter which would brook no argument and to her own surprise she found herself meekly trading off, with a colleague, a precious Saturday for today's leave. But equally she told herself, 'This is the last concession I make for you, Stefan Radulescu.'

What should she wear? She'd agonised over the choice of clothes. He'd caught her on the hop—there hadn't been time to shop for a new outfit.

'Nothing too casual or flighty that's likely to put a cantankerous lawyer's back up and nothing too dowdy so that he assumed he could push her around,' she decided. And even she was comfortable with the compromise—a creamy, silk shirt with a peter-pan collar curving over the turquoise edge-to-edge jacket and a circular calf-length matching skirt which swung about her sheer stockinged legs below a waist-clinching belt. Her thick, shiny hair was caught back in a broad, black grosgrain bow, revealing gold stud ear-rings, a present from uncle last Christmas.

The stark white walls on both sides of the main entrance door bore in black gloss paint the names of all the barristers who had a seat in chambers, that of Stefan Radulescu Q.C. heading the list. Gemma's heart sank. He sounded very important and it could only mean one thing—he was head of chambers. Worse and worse. She steeled herself and approached the clerk's desk.

'Conference with counsel?' He was a dapper man with ginger hair and thick spectacles.

The unfamiliar jargon confused her, 'Er, um . . . I believe I'm expected. I have an appointment with Mr Radulescu,' she added hastily, her heart thudding slightly as she mentioned her name. The moment she'd been waiting for all those weeks had arrived at last and she felt so excited, it was almost unbearable.

'Hmm,' he consulted a list, running a finger down it. 'Right here we are—Miss Wells, four p.m. Follow me please.'

Her well-polished brown court shoes clattered on the steep flight of wooden stairs that led to an upper floor. The clerk pushed open a door on the carpeted landing. 'Wait in here, please. Mr Radulescu will be with you shortly.'

Gemma crossed the large room and gazed down into the courtyard, the silence of the Inn interrupted only by the muted voices of robed and bewigged figures scurrying across it earnestly discussing points of law. Two hours ago, it had seemed easy enough. It would be just a formality, a simple explanation in layman's language, nothing to worry about. But now she wondered if she ought to have limited it to a verbal discussion—the

43

telephone would have done as well. The suspense was almost overwhelming. She forced herself to sit in one of the high-backed red hide armchairs and looked around. It was a plain room dominated by a massive mahogany desk strewn with briefs wound round with lawyers' pink tape. A clock in the French Empire style stood on the Carrara marble mantelpiece and a sombre portrait of a judge in ceremonial robes hung from one off-white wall. Orderly, cold, the room was curiously devoid of personal touches.

Gemma glanced impatiently at her watch. He had kept her waiting almost half an hour. 'If he isn't here within the next five minutes, I'm leaving,' she resolved. It wasn't a very auspicious beginning.

Then she heard the unmistakable sound of stairs being mounted two at a time and unconsciously braced herself for the encounter. The door burst open and Gemma's prepared greeting froze on her lips. The man facing her, although partially transformed by his yellowing horse-hair wig, was patently the man from the storm—the one person she'd never expected to meet again.

It was as much a surprise to him as it was to her. He paused. 'This is a miracle,' he exclaimed, 'if only you knew how much I wanted—I was about to—' he checked himself. His green eyes darkened as they rested on her face and almost immediately he recovered himself.

He said drily, 'Are you as floored as you look by the long arm of coincidence?' He did not seem to want a reply and the sudden expression of joy in his eyes was just as suddenly veiled. His broad shoulders shrugged off the long, black gown and his handshake was firm as the long fingers closed over hers.

'As you can see I was detained in court.' She supposed it was meant to be an apology although he didn't sound particularly sorry but then she would hardly have expected that from the man from the storm.

'*You're* Stefan Radulescu!' she exclaimed involuntarily, utterly dismayed.

'I'm sure I am,' his tone was amused. He tossed the wig aside, his black hair springy beneath it.

'And I know who you must be but first just a few formalities for the record.' He flung himself into a swivel chair and his tone became cool, professional. He jotted down her replies in a ruled, blue-backed counsel's notebook. He certainly didn't waste time on social niceties Gemma thought, nor did he offer her refreshment as if to emphasise to her that this was not a social occasion. Strangely enough this heightened her sense of anticipation.

'I believe you know you are the principal beneficiary, Miss Wells?' He lowered his head slightly, linking his arms behind his head.

Gemma sat facing him separated by the

45

desk. Put like that she thought it took on a whole new, awesome meaning.

'Tell me,' he said, a note of concern in his voice, 'did you manage to arrive that day without further mishap?'

'Indeed, I did, thanks to you,' she said somewhat primly, trying not to remember the familiar exchanges and blushing as she did so.

She groped for words, her voice a croak, 'Did . . . did you know who I was that night?'

A puzzled expression drifted across his face, 'How could I? This—' a strong, shapely hand motioned 'is as much a surprise to you as it is to me. I never dreamt I'd see—' he broke off and then as if reading her mind he added gently, 'so despite what you may think, I had no ulterior motive in delaying this meeting—merely pressure of work.'

Gemma felt small and let it pass. In his dark, expensively tailored jacket and black pin-striped trousers he looked a formidable advocate. She hoped he was not going to be as formidable a trustee.

Stefan undid his stiff white neck bands with a flick of his wrist and slid them across the desk. 'Ah—that's better—dreadfully uncomfortable things.' The gesture was oddly disturbing.

He leaned forward slightly, rolling a heavy gold pen between his fingers and studied her for a moment. She looked hastily away, feeling uncomfortable.

'Hanson has outlined the terms of the Will to you I gather?' he asked, his jawline hard. His businesslike manner helped restore her composure.

Gemma nodded, 'Yes, he gave me a copy of it.'

'And the original is now in my possession, although I don't think it will be necessary for me to refer to it at present.'

Gemma doubted if he ever would need to. He was the sort of man who would have memorised it at a glance.

'So there is no need for me to repeat that your uncle has left you a very tidy sum.' He scribbled some figures on a piece of paper and pushed it towards her. 'This is subject to confirmation, after a formal valuation of his estate, but it does give you some indication . . .'

Gemma gasped, 'I had . . . had . . . no idea,' she stammered. Had uncle really amassed such wealth as a self-made man? He had lived comfortably but without ostentation. True, Moore chauffeured him around in the black Daimler but Uncle had bought that ten years ago and he often told her that as it did the job it was designed to do very nicely there was no need for him to change it for the latest model.

'That was Arthur's general idea,' Stefan smiled unexpectedly. He continued: 'In this,' he pointed to a letter in front of him and Gemma could just, by reading upside down, make out her uncle's no-nonsense

47

handwriting. 'Arthur describes the conditions you must satisfy to enable the capital of the trust fund to be released to you.'

He gave her a long, thoughtful look, leaning back in his chair so that it tilted on its castors, a man totally at ease.

Gemma leaned forward, her arms on the desk, wishing she felt as relaxed, her blue eyes very large.

'What did Uncle mean by "satisfy"? Satisfy whom?'

'Me,' Stefan said softly, 'as the trustee.'

'But how—in what way?' She interjected, shifting uneasily in her chair.

'I'm coming to that—if you'll be kind enough to permit me,' he said quietly.

Gemma subsided back in the chair, her fingers gripping the armrests, raking her memory for any clues to Uncle Arthur's intentions.

'It's quite simple. He wants you to run your own business—let me finish,' Stefan firmly quashed her attempts to interrupt him again. 'You're free to select any activity you like provided I approve and vet it. If I think it sounds workable, I have the discretion, which I will exercise, to make you an advance of five thousand pounds to start you off to enable you to buy whatever equipment you need. And every month I will expect you to show me an analysis of your monthly takings so that I can monitor your progress. If at the end of six months I'm satisfied that your business is on its way to becoming a profitable, going concern, then the capital of the fund and "Four Winds" will be transferred to you outright.'

He reached out a hand and opened a brief. Gemma registered the implications, unaware of the look of growing distaste on her face. She was securely settled in a reasonably well paid job coasting along with her own comfortable flat and a wide circle of friends. She was not going to throw all that up for some risky venture.

'It's quite outrageous,' she expostulated finally. 'I don't want to run my own business. I'm quite happy as I am. If I'd wanted to go into business, I'd have taken a business management course. It's utterly ridiculous. I can't think what possessed him.' She was flushed, her thoughts chaotic. She nearly said that Uncle must have been unhinged but caught herself in time, appalled at the direction of her thoughts.

Stefan looked up, 'Unpredictable, eccentric maybe but Arthur was definitely not lunatic,' he said bluntly.

'What happens if I refuse?' Gemma asked suddenly. His green eyes clashed with hers, 'If you refuse or your business fails because you haven't done your best (and I'll be the judge of that) then you'll have to repay the five thousand pounds and you'll get nothing of the capital. The inheritance will be distributed between your distant cousins and various charities. So—it's all or nothing. Will you take it on?' There was a questioning glint in his eyes.

Gemma lifted her chin, 'No, I won't even consider it.' It would put paid to her independence. She'd be locked into something from which there could be no easy escape. How can you just start a business and expect it to run itself? she asked herself. It would perpetuate itself—expand, proliferate and then there'd be accountants, solicitors, salesmen and ad-men. She didn't want to compete for any awards. No—she was absolutely positive—it was not her scene.

'I should have thought it was a challenge you couldn't resist.' Again the glint lit his eyes.

Gemma struggled with arising tide of rage. This man for whom it seemed everything fell effortlessly into his lap—what did he know about challenges?

'My present job is challenge enough,' she retorted swiftly.

Stefan looked sceptical and raised one dark eyebrow. She burst out, 'This . . . so-called business proposition. It's an unwarranted intrusion into my life. If you want a challenge, then you shall have it.' She paused, the expression on his face was unreadable. 'I shall contest this bizarre trust. I'll take this absurd Will to court.'

She jumped to her feet and picked up her

shoulder-bag. He watched her for a moment, 'Stop flapping, Gemma and sit down.' There was a ring of authority in his voice that made her hesitate.

'You are, of course, free to do as you wish but I wouldn't advise it. You're unlikely to win. Arthur was no fool—he was shrewd enough to seek my opinion on the validity of the trust before he set it up.'

Gemma was still on her feet. 'And I suppose you assured him there was no way round it?' A tinge of sarcasm crept into her tone. 'Well that's not good enough for me. That's just one lawyer's view—*your* view. Another barrister might well think it's worth fighting.'

He pushed back his chair and stood up. He came round to her side of the desk and sat on the edge of it and looked at her, his arms folded across his chest.

His voice was unexpectedly gentle, 'Don't waste money you haven't got in that way. Think about it. It's possible, you know, that your uncle may have seen more in you than you see yourself. I'm not rushing you.' He touched her arm and the contact made her shiver with sudden arousal. Abruptly she drew away, angry with herself for feeling like this when rational thought told her she had every reason to dislike this man who was turning her world upside down.

Gemma breathed hard as she tried to reassert control.

'I don't need to have any second thoughts. I don't want or need time. Fine, you're the expert—'the courts will uphold the Will. But that doesn't alter things. I won't agree—I can't,' she broke off, swallowing painfully, her body taut.

'So, you're afraid. It boils down to that. Who would have thought it?' he said wonderingly, shaking his head.

She could almost hear the blood pounding through her veins. He was determined, clever—using all his lawyer's tricks to manoeuvre her into something which simply held no appeal.

'What have I got to be scared of?' She had ceased her angry pacing of his room, her confidence in herself unshaken.

'What have you got to lose?' he urged her, 'using the same gutsiness to make a go of it as you're doing to resist it, it's bound to be a winner.' His green eyes travelled slowly over her.

She let that one go before answering. 'I don't want to discuss it any further,' she said wearily, more than ready for home. As far as she was concerned the subject was closed.

Stefan walked to the door as he spoke, 'I expect all this has come as somewhat as a shock to you so I'm quite prepared to give you as long as you need to reconsider your decision.'

Gemma didn't reply, aware that she had

flared up rather more than was justified. His hand was on the door knob as he held it open for her. Unaccountably, her bag slipped from her shoulder.

'Oh.' She stooped to pick it up as he did, too. Their eyes met and the veiled green eyes were sharp, making her feel suddenly very exposed. She lowered her lashes and straightened up, feeling a slight tug round her neck. The long gold chain she wore outside her blouse had entangled itself round one of the buttons on his starched white shirt.

'Allow me,' Stefan's voice was laced with amusement. He was maddeningly slow, his fingers brushing against her breasts and all the time she was so close she could hear the steady beating of his heart and smell the tang of his aftershave. At last the chain fell free.

'Thanks,' she mumbled, her face crimson with discomfiture.

'*Au revoir*, Gemma—until the next time.'

'There isn't going to be a next time,' she smiled faintly, intent on avoiding any more encounters with this dark, dangerous man. The score was even now and nothing must be allowed to alter the balance between them. He ignored her thrust and she could feel his eyes flickering over her as she descended the stairs.

*   *   *

Gemma kicked off her shoes and dropped

53

onto the deeply-cushioned sofa. Assorted silken tassels and yards of curtaining fabric washed over the small, pine dining-table. She felt stupidly guilty that she hadn't yet started on the cutting out. The grind of home-going traffic along the A2 drifted faintly across to her top floor flat overlooking Blackheath which centuries ago had been the mustering point for the Peasants' Revolt.

A glass of gin and tonic topped by a twist of lemon at her elbow, she idly turned the pages of the glossy magazine she had picked up on impulse from her local newsagent. The racks were full of similar ones beguilingly entitled 'Be Your Own Boss' and 'Run Your Own Business'. Not that she had the slightest intention of doing so . . . But as a librarian, she told herself, she was duty-bound to amass as much information as she could, however uninteresting it was to her personally. Popular, booming, a growth area—the clichés leapt from the page. But it's not for me—not even when there's so much at stake, she thought. The prospect of having to sell herself made her shudder with revulsion. She read with horror one reader's desperate letter to the editor. He ran a computer programming outfit—his customers didn't pay promptly and he was sick with worry over things like cashflow, budgets and pressing creditors.

Gemma swung her legs onto the pale green carpet, her brain in top gear, rehearsing the mature, considered refusal she would send to Stefan. Then it would be finito and with a bit of luck he would have the grace to leave her alone. A colour photograph of a de luxe knitting machine which she'd always rather coveted caught her eye. Its owner, a lively looking woman in her early thirties described herself as a reluctant shopkeeper. With a suddenly invalided husband and three children under the age of five, she found herself the main breadwinner; she turned her hobby into a profitable concern and was now set to diversify into mail orders. What began as a small cottage industry had become, after a bumpy start, a thriving small business.

Gemma read the feature again more slowly and took the magazine with her into the country-style kitchen, from which she could see the elegant spire of the parish church. She set a lamb chop to grill and assembled a salad— lettuce, tomatoes, yesterday's boiled potatoes, capsicum, a large dollop of Feta cheese tossed with classic French dressing in a garlic smeared hickory bowl. She chewed thoughtfully. She hardly cared to admit it to herself, least of all to Stefan, but things were fraught at work. Her old affable supervisor had retired to be replaced by a slick, power hungry younger man. Their clashes were frequent and wearing but what with the cut-backs in the library service and the fierce competition for rarely occurring vacancies, Gemma's plans to move on had come badly unstuck.

*   *   *

'I've decided to resign and do my own thing,' Gemma told Pip casually, nicely judging the sensation her announcement would cause.

Pip opened and closed her mouth like a beached whale.

'Out on your own?' she demanded incredulously, 'I just have to meet your Stefan—what powers of persuasion!' Knowing Gemma's enthusiasm for the community library, her change of mind seemed utterly unbelievable.

'It was my decision, and he's not my Stefan. It has nothing at all to do with him,' Gemma said crossly. 'Today Blackheath, tomorrow the world.'

Pip choked down a friendly retort, 'It must have been his sexy foreign accent. Ooh,' she purred.

'Far from it—he couldn't sound less foreign if he tried. Now which of my many skills is going to unlock the door to fame and fortune?' she tried to change the subject, wishing Pip would forget about Stefan.

'But he was foreign originally?' Pip pursued relentlessly and Gemma saw that her friend was determined to endow him with mystery and glamour.

'We didn't get around to discussing that,'

Gemma said quickly.

Pip looked disappointed, 'There you are, another golden opportunity lost. You should be quicker off the mark. Now if I were in your shoes . . .'

'If you were me,' Gemma seized on her last remark, 'what product or services would you sell?'

'Well the proof of the meringues is in the eating and, as you're not exactly Delia Smith, you can forget catering,' she reminded her friend bluntly.

Gemma giggled, remembering her recent disasters in the kitchen. 'Stefan has to sanction it.' She sighed and chewed the end of her pencil.

Pip pulled a face, the swashbuckling character she'd built Stefan up into faded to a school-masterly figure.

'Listen,' Gemma doodled in her notepad and frowned in concentration, 'what do you think of this . . . ?'

She spent the rest of that afternoon bouncing her list of business ideas off Pip.

'There are so many things I could do,' she enthused, 'that in next to no time, I'll have not one, but several businesses on the go.'

*   *   *

The Honda scraped to a halt by the kerb. Gemma walked briskly into the clerk's room.

He gave her a beady look as he pulled on his overcoat. Reluctantly he keyed into Stefan's extension.

'Like me, he's just ready to go for the day, Miss Wells, but he says he can give you a few minutes,' he reported grudgingly.

The penalty of arriving unannounced, Gemma thought, feeling a little disgruntled as she thanked the clerk. 'It's all right, I know the way.' She deposited her crash helmet at the foot of the stairs, raking fingers through her hair.

She got the feeling that Stefan was annoyed about something, his green eyes points of ice as he watched her in a small shaving-mirror propped up on the mantelpiece as he knotted his black bow tie. He looked devastatingly attractive in evening dress, the long body at ease in the formal suit, immaculate black trousers a perfect fit over the flat stomach.

Her hands curled into fists in the pocket of her loose, Fair Isle cardigan, 'I've decided to start my own business.'

He appraised her coolly, his reaction unexpectedly indifferent, 'What specifically do you have in mind?' he asked evenly and Gemma, who had expected her decision to be greeted with enthusiasm, felt chilled. Had he no idea what it had cost her? She had looked forward to describing to him what had prompted her to take the plunge. She felt suddenly very despondent.

'Can you spare the time?' Disappointment made her voice sound clipped.

'To be perfectly honest—no. I'm about to leave for the opera but now that you're here, do go on.' Stefan gave her a polite smile. His eyes moved thoughtfully over her as he registered the scuffed trainers, the long legs and rounded bottom moulded in the skin-tight jeans, the swelling curves of her breasts.

Unfeeling swine, Gemma thought illogically, quite forgetting she had called by unannounced. Who would want to hear the grandeur of the music with him? It was quite unreasonable, ridiculous, but she felt a sudden unnerving spurt of jealousy.

Without waiting to be asked, she sat down and flung her leather jacket over the back of the chair. Okay, she admitted it, he had strong sexual magnetism, and looking at him now as he deftly slid gold links into his shirt cuffs, she knew he was a supreme opportunist and would push his male advantage mercilessly.

'Graphic art—you know, designing cards and posters,' Gemma struck out boldly. At school she had been considered talented and she'd won a number of art prizes.

There was a stunned silence, 'You're not serious.' His green eyes considered her. She continued 'There's a real gap in the market. You've only got to look around to see the demand. None of the stuff on sale's of high quality. Mine will be different—unique,

59

contemporary, witty . . .'

'Forget it,' Stefan said trenchantly. Rage began to bubble up inside her. 'Why?' she demanded. 'Give me one good reason. What do you know about it anyway?' Her blue eyes glittered.

'Look,' Stefan drew up a chair, and crossed one silk socked leg over the other, 'you haven't done your homework. The industry is badly under employed. There's a chronic shortage of work.' He paused and flicked a lighter, 'There's no way you can make a living from that.'

'I'm positive I could,' Gemma said doggedly, totally hooked now by the spirit of enterprise. 'It's a challenge—you said so yourself. A daring adventure.'

The rich aroma of Havana filled the air, 'An ordeal, more likely. You'll have to come up with something less fanciful.'

Gemma grinned suddenly, mischievously. He couldn't think she was naïve enough not to have put together a package of alternatives.

'I have other proposals under consideration . . .' she said loftily, feeling oddly triumphant.

*   *   *

The telephone shrilled, making her jump. Stefan tapped white cigar ash into a chunky ashtray then reached across and depressed the loudspeaker button.

'Darling!' a woman's voice breathed huskily. 'We have a date—remember?'

She sounded so close to Gemma that she might have been there standing in the room. Gemma could almost picture her enveloped in a heady cloud of perfume, a blonde mink jacket draped casually about her shoulders.

'How could I forget?' His voice was warm, sensuous—lacking the briskness with which he had addressed Gemma. She stood up, feeling awkward, as if she had eavesdropped on a lovers' private conversation, but Stefan waved her back into her seat. She hesitated.

'Please sit down,' he repeated mildly.

Gemma sat down on the edge of her chair. She couldn't afford to antagonise him, unpleasant though it was to have to do as he asked.

'Is there someone with you?' The caller's voice was smooth, amused.

'Not for long.'

'Then I can relax, knowing you're on the way.'

'And so shall I—in pursuit of the divine.'

The response pleased her for she gave a low gurgle of laughter before there was a click of the receiver being replaced.

Gemma felt very flat and somehow dejected. She heard Stefan's voice as if through a haze.

'So—you've thought ahead?' He was looking across at her, raising his black

61

eyebrows. 'What foresight.'

'I thought of driving a minicab—you know, undercutting taxi fares over long distances . . .' she managed to keep her voice even.

'You won't live to collect,' he said succinctly. 'Next one?'

He listened patiently but was equally dismissive of selling antiques, 'the other dealers will rip you off,' and gently dissuaded her from curtain and blind-making.

'Good ideas are two a penny,' he stubbed out his cigar, 'you have to aim to collect a steady stream of paying customers and to pitch your price so that you make a clear profit,' he advised candidly.

'So much for turning a hobby into a business,' Gemma stormed bitterly, 'you're being deliberately obstructive. I thought you wanted me to do this. Now you're being totally inconsistent.' She glared at the top of his dark, well-groomed head. She didn't care if he was seeing her at her worst.

In the silence that followed the outburst she wondered if he had registered her remarks. Would he say that she was unfit to run her own show? Tell her to go back to the library?

Stefan's mouth twitched, 'You'll have to control that hot temper if you want to exploit your entrepreneurial flair.'

'You mean, it's still on?' she brushed away the tears of angry frustration that gleamed on her lashes.

He hoisted her into his arms, 'I want you to make it as much as you do,' he said. There was an odd inflection in his tone. Gemma stifled a harsh sob and he closed in on her stroking her hair as she cried into his pleated shirt, not caring if it was ruined by damp mascara. The strong pressure of his arms was reassuring, and a languorous warmth flowed through her. She lifted her face, her throat swollen with salt.

'I'm all right now,' she muttered and sniffed, still feeling fragile. He was still holding her. He produced a large silk handkerchief and proceeded to dry her face, doing it so gently that it was a struggle to keep her tears at bay.

Gemma drew away, 'You'll be late for your date.' Her colour was a hectic flush.

'And that won't do. I couldn't bear to hear another woman cry,' he said blandly with a teasing sweep of his long, dark lashes.

'That's not very funny,' she said stiffly, only too aware of the sight she must present—shiny nose and tearstained face.

He directed her to an adjoining bathroom and she splashed her face with cold water. It was very unlike her, she thought as she stared at her dishevelled, disturbed reflection. She'd never considered herself an emotional type but now, all of a sudden, her life was filled with new and unknown shadows.

*   *   *

Some days later she saw Stefan on the television news exiting rapidly from the Old Bailey as his delighted client, a flamboyant financier, walked free after a headline-making fraud trial. Gemma gave a little gasp, suddenly quite weak at the knees as she watched Stefan fend off the press with consummate skill. He was a clever, dangerous man to tangle with and the thought sent curious shivers up and down her spine.

*   *   *

Now as she bent over the bike, sleeves rolled to the elbows, an image of Stefan's strong face floated before her and she knew there would be more problems as much from his side as from herself.

'Well, there's nothing like hard, physical work to clear the brain,' Gemma supposed. She applied a little more turtle wax to the bodywork, buffing and polishing it with a yellow duster until her arms ached. She stood back, her legs apart, hands on hips and admired her handiwork. The queen of the road, she thought proudly. Its chrome gleamed in the March sunshine under a crocus-blue sky. She was sorely tempted to abandon other household chores, to race down to the coast, forget her worries, real and make-believe and then roar back home to a meal and a drink.

The solution was there—right under her

nose—so obvious that she could hardly believe it hadn't occurred to her earlier. She grabbed her helmet and sped round to Pip's flat, her body curved excitedly over her bike.

People would want something a little different—it couldn't fail. Stefan would have to back it—she was determined he would.

*   *   *

'Brilliant,' Pip enthused as she handed Gemma a mug of coffee, 'motor-cycle holidays in England, all arranged, nothing for the bikers to do but to relax. Stefan'll be mad to turn it down. If he does, I'll go round personally and brain him with this.' She swung her helmet above her head with a battle cry.

'That's far too precious to waste on him,' Gemma protested, her eyes dancing with excitement.

Several days and lightning phone calls later, and reinforced with tips from the government sponsored small firms' service, Gemma had perfected her blueprint.

*   *   *

Gemma found it difficult to concentrate on her violin practice that morning. She flexed her arm and readjusted the angle of the bow, tucking the instrument under her chin. But the strings sounded colourless and vapid when the score called for a boisterous, lively rondo.

'Bother,' she thought, accidentally knocking over the music stand as she moved restlessly. Early morning sunlight flooded across the heath making the well-loved furniture look rather worn. She half sighed and tried to return to her music. The doorbell rang; once, twice. She frowned slightly. Her elderly neighbour had taken to inviting himself up on the pretext of being a music lover but this time she decided to ignore him. It was just eight o'clock—far too early in the day to be entertaining him. She had to practise this piece until it was perfect, or risk expulsion from the local orchestra. She turned the pages of the score, skipping the hard bits, promising herself to go back over them.

'Persistent so and so,' Gemma swore cheerfully as the bell continued to ring, as if the caller's finger was glued to it. She set down her violin and padded into the hall, half-resigned, half-relieved at the interruption. She knew she didn't have the heart to turn him away. Since the sudden death of his wife, he had looked baffled—lonely and frailer.

'I was beginning to think I was interrupting something,' the deep voice said wryly. Stefan lounged against the doorpost, hands thrust in the pockets of his cream corduroy trousers streamlining the hard, muscled body. The broad shoulders moved under a soft, leather blouson, the colour of milk chocolate. He looked fresh, alert.

Stunned, Gemma stared at him. He was the last person she would have expected on her doorstep at that hour of the morning, and the shock of it almost made the breath catch in her throat.

Abruptly she said, 'Well, you are, but it's not what you probably had in mind.' She ushered him in and he registered at a glance her love of gardening in the hanging and potted plants which adorned every room.

'And what do you think I had in mind?' His gaze burned across her, dropping from the cloud of red hair to the curves beneath the silk polka-dot dressing-gown. An odd tightening of her stomach made her suddenly tongue-tied, noting his wide sensual mouth and the masterly assurance of his body.

She recovered herself quickly, 'What ninety-five per cent of men think about ninety-five per cent of the time.' Her gaze was very direct and she was sure from the expression on his face that he knew what she meant.

Stefan burst out laughing, 'How charmingly non-specific. Don't you know it's sex, money and love that make the world go round?'

Gemma gave him a hard stare and went into the kitchen. He followed, watching her as she set the kettle to boil and took some rashers of bacon out of the fridge. 'How absolutely riveting. Is that in increasing or decreasing order of priority?' She was angry with herself for letting him provoke her but was unable to do anything about it. She sensed a slight tension in his frame but his eyes, veiled behind the dark lashes, gave nothing away.

'Very good, very neat.' Then he pounced, 'Well you'll be able to judge for yourself as our association becomes closer, as undoubtedly it will.' He gave her a swift slanted look which held amusement. At that moment, she couldn't have detested him more. He was infuriatingly ambiguous, utterly hateful, quick to seize the psychological advantage. She wished she'd had the sense to ignore his opening gambit. He'd wrong-footed her and she ought to have been prepared for it with a man like Stefan. She pretended to be engrossed with the eggs, cracking them carefully into a bowl before she tipped them into the frying-pan.

'What could be closer or nicer than tea for two?' There was a glint of mischief in his eyes as he took the tray from her.

Gemma began to laugh, 'Do you always shoot from the hip?'

'Not guilty,' Stefan assured her with mock solemnity as he carried the tray into the sitting-room.

Gemma bit back a retort and decided to accept the remark at face value.

'Now where do you want this?' he answered the question himself, 'over here.' He deposited the tray on a table by the window from which on that clear morning Gemma could see the faint outline of Greenwich Royal Observatory.

'Orion, Cygnus and Aquila—they're all still suspended out there somewhere,' he tackled the meal with relish, as if it had been a long time since he'd eaten anything, oblivious to the shrivelled rashers of bacon and the charred sausage.

'What?' Gemma paused, her fork half way to her mouth, wondering if she'd misheard him. She glanced at his face which suddenly looked very serious.

'The stars—that vault of heaven. Do you know that out there there are meteor showers, galaxies, cosmic fields beyond our wildest imaginings?'

She thought she detected a yearning note in Stefan's voice as if the search for his own private world, his own heaven, still eluded him. She felt a painful lump in her throat at the unexpected personal exposure. Quasars, pulsars, terrestrial forces, she knew nothing of this, but his personal magnetism was real, potent. An electric shiver coursed through her but that brief glimpse of him—human, vulnerable, dissolved as quickly as it had surfaced and for a moment she wondered if it had been a trick of the senses.

'The observatory has a powerful telescope,' he explained as he spread orange marmalade over lavishly buttered toast. If he always ate so heartily Gemma thought, it was amazing how he managed to retain that lean, muscular look.

'This is delicious,' he took an appreciative bite. Gemma broke free from the poignancy of the moment, raw and elemental, which held her captive. She shot him a look of disbelief, 'But the public can't use it can they?'

There was a boyish gleam in his green eyes, 'I'm one of those perfectly dreadful people who can pull strings, so I'm allowed to beam it up, after dark. I've been there overnight, tracking the sky.' He had re-asserted his authority, subtly, naturally. 'And since you're within walking distance, I decided to pay a visit to your nerve centre.'

'So you're a super nova.' She couldn't resist the impulse to cloak the dull ache of disappointment which swept over her. Yet she knew it was ridiculous, foolish of her to suppose that he had deliberately sought her out. Why should he? After all his interest, if it could be called that, in her was purely professional.

He neatly side-stepped the implication. 'Surely that aim should be uppermost in your thoughts?' he asked slyly, the shrewd eyes fixed on her face.

Gemma's cheeks burned with the sudden realisation of how unguarded her face must look, but his dry smile teased out the sting. She dabbed her mouth with a table napkin and stood up.

'Speedwell Holidays,' she announced briskly. She flung him a covert look from under her lashes. The idea once born had been christened instantly, almost superstitiously as if that would make it proof against failure.

'Go on,' Stefan shifted in his chair and slapped the table top with his palm, his eyes bright with interest.

'I've thought it all out—it's all in here,' Gemma swivelled on her bare heels and produced her carefully researched report with its colour-coded charts and computer projections.

Stefan registered the painstaking analysis with a smiling glance at her, his legs stretched out across the carpet, the fabric of his trousers tight across the muscles of his thighs. He looked relaxed and a warm, relaxed feeling began to float over her.

'And since I know the locale, I'll prepare a leaflet describing all the interesting places, the wildlife, the scenery, smells and sounds within a fifty-mile radius. I'll do all the tiresome legwork like booking the accommodation in small rural hotels so that all the bikers need do is roam about at their own pace and return to a convivial meal.' Gemma scanned Stefan's face anxiously under level brows, trying to gauge his reaction.

'Good try,' he said casually, almost too casually. She felt startled, 'You mean you'll buy it?' she gasped, surprise making her feel dazed, almost light-headed.

'I hope plenty do,' he laughed deep inside

his chest. 'I approve unreservedly. Are you surprised?' For a moment his fingers were on her chin, warm and strong.

'Yes—very,' Gemma admitted, still hardly able to believe her luck. She began to stack the crockery and the bright red hair swung forward as her head bent. 'I felt as if I'd never win you over—it was beginning to be like the twelve labours of Hercules.' She allowed a trace of grimness to tinge her tone. 'I never expected this. You seemed so exacting.'

He took the laden tray from her and carried it to the sink and, although he insisted, she refused to let him wash up. He wandered back into her sitting-room and examined a small framed poster explosive with shape and colour.

'You make me sound like an archetypal trustee,' he said ruefully. He swung round suddenly, 'And I promise to be one.'

She searched his green eyes tensely, then caught the chuckle under his growl and began to laugh, and the anxious moment evaporated.

'Now, before I forget,' Stefan yanked out his cheque book, completed the words and figures with thick, dark gashes and tore out the cheque. 'That's the *loan* I promised you.' He had no intention of letting her forget.

Gemma nodded vigorously, her eyes shining. She folded it in two, and slipped it into her dressing-gown pocket. It was all beginning to happen.

She saw Stefan to the door and he put a lazy

arm round her. For one wild moment, she thought he was going to kiss her and her body leapt in response. His eyes were intent on her lips; his dark head came closer and she slid her arms round his neck, naturally, instinctively. He eased them down gently, his expression ironic. He must have known how much she wanted his embrace—the occasion called for it—and had quite deliberately, coolly denied her. Yet for a moment she had thought that he had wanted it too.

'Don't squander it on champagne and loose living,' he said cheerfully, as if oblivious to her pain, but there was a warning edge to his tone.

She heard his footsteps descending the stairs and moved dully to the window, breathing in the fresh, morning air. He glanced up as he unlocked his car—not the Volvo Gemma noticed, but a sleek, silver Jaguar XJ6—his town car, she supposed.

'Thank you for a magnificent breakfast, Gemma,' he called out wickedly in a voice pitched at an invisible audience. He made it sound like an orgy. She grimaced and ducked back hastily. Was he always to have the last word in that insouciant way?

CHAPTER THREE

It was May, the time of year Gemma loved the best but that day its magic was not working. She sighed and leaned across the window-seat resting her elbows on the sill. Her mood seemed to match the grey clouds hanging over the fields that sloped away from the grounds of Glenside Hall Hotel. How had the bikers spent their day out in the rain, she wondered, biting her lower lip anxiously. She hardly dared think about it, but no matter what she did, what routine she manufactured for herself, the worry was there like a numbing headache. It was a complete disaster, she was sure of that. She dreaded their return—irritable and damp, grumpily revving their engines and frightening the cattle grazing in the lush green meadows. There would be loud remarks about how their hard-earned cash would have been better spent at the Isle of Man T.T. The news would spread like wildfire among the entire biking fraternity, she would be boycotted and . . . Gemma shuddered. It was too horrible to contemplate. She might as well pack it in now and go back to library work before bankruptcy descended on her. There was no disgrace in having tried and failed. Stefan was bound to accept that, or would he? Her stomach lurched as an image of his hard, leanly muscled body flashed before her eyes. She ran a distracted hand across her curls, as the sound of a ship's handbell, rung impatiently, echoed eerily through the deserted vestibule.

'Hello! Anyone there?' Heavy footsteps sounded on the polished wood floor.

Gemma swung round, her face breaking into a smile.

'Bruce! What a lovely surprise! What brings you here?' Her gloom and sense of isolation lifted as she recognised the tall, tanned man with the smooth blond hair.

'I'm driving up to Edinburgh on business. Pip said you were holed up here, so I thought I'd drop by to see how the new venture's coming along—give you the benefit of my expertise.' His eyes as blue as her own swept appreciatively over her long-limbed body clad in black leather trousers over which she wore a multi-coloured tee-shirt.

'It's great to see you,' Gemma said warmly, impulsively kissing him on the cheek. It felt cool and smooth. 'Come on, sit down. Can I offer you a drink?'

Bruce shook his head and sank into a squashy armchair, unbuttoning the jacket of his elegant Italian-made suit. 'Not at the moment, thanks. I say, do you think they'll be able to fit me in here?'

'I don't think they're full up. My lot's occupying eight bedrooms and it's advertised as a ten-room place, so you're in luck,' she said

75

cheerfully. It was good to see Bruce and even better that he planned to stay for a few days. A friend of Pip's brother Richard, Bruce was a link with home ground. That and his own oozing self-confidence had already begun to rub off on her, dissipating the anxieties which had beset her since the bikers' arrival. And he was a businessman himself—the director of a flourishing investment company in the City. She could unburden herself and he would understand. Unlike Stefan, she thought, who had been cold comfort so far.

Bruce raised one pale eyebrow, 'How are things anyway? I hear you're doing a roaring trade.' His eyes never left her face.

Gemma laughed and crossed from the window to the chair opposite him. 'Wishful thinking—Pip's hyperbole, as usual. It's early days yet.' She was conscious that she had begun to relax, confident that, with Bruce's moral support, she would be able more easily to mollify any aggrieved bikers.

He waggled a finger at her, 'The first rule of business is to think success. Never aim low or you'll hit it,' he chided her loftily.

He glanced round the homely furnished lounge with its glass fronted cases crammed with *objets d'art*, its polished oak floor and scatter rugs in glowing colours.

'Not bad. Strikes the right note. Not too bargain basement and not too palatial. The acceptable middle ground. How did you find

76

it?' He sounded curious.

'Purely by accident,' Gemma confessed to her unbusinesslike approach. 'I literally stumbled on it.' Bruce shook with mirth as she gave a graphic account of how she'd discovered the ivy-covered baronial-style sandstone house behind a thick screen of dark green conifers. It seemed the perfect spot— rambling, yet not impersonal, standing in its own large grounds amidst the rolling countryside of the Scottish-English borders.

In Bruce's company, Gemma felt at ease and unselfconscious. It contrasted dramatically with how she reacted in Stefan's presence. He made her feel as if her emotions were being stretched like a piece of elastic.

'Seriously, though,' Bruce unloosened his designer tie which matched perfectly the thin yellow stripe in his suit. 'I hope the rest of your business plan is not as haphazard as that.' His deep voice with its transatlantic undertones acquired from frequent forays to New York was admonishing. 'I'm going to teach you a few things you wouldn't learn at Harvard Business School.' He smiled in a way that suggested to her that he didn't intend to talk business with her for long. 'Now, for a start, how are you going to keep your customers entertained?'

He listened intently to her ideas, his smooth head tilted in interest. Stefan, Stefan, Gemma thought gleefully, if only you could see me now. Having Bruce around was a tonic, a comforting bulwark. Bruce was direct, positive and genuinely interested in her venture. It was more—much more than anyone could hope or expect from a friend. And Bruce was hardly that, as yet, as she knew him only through his connection with Richard. And Bruce was so affable. Gemma couldn't help resist making the comparison with Stefan who made her prickle and placed all those obstacles in her path. Damn the man, she thought furiously, couldn't she banish him from her thoughts even at a time like this?

'Brilliant.' Bruce's eyes darted past her to his red Porsche drawn up on the grass verge. 'I'll have to shift that before your lot gets back. Is there a garage?'

The glow Gemma felt from his approval faded. 'You don't need to worry about it. It's quite safe. We aren't thugs, you know, just because we wear leather,' she protested acidly.

His eyes narrowed, then he laughed off the awkward moment. 'You look anything but a thug in that. Vroom, vroom. More like a *femme fatale.*'

Gemma felt the colour rise in her cheeks but didn't avert her gaze.

'Now listen.' He changed the subject, slipping back easily into his self-appointed business consultant role. 'As I drove over here, I saw some magnificent empty stretches of land—just the place for a scramble. What do you think? That'll get them going. After all, variety's the spice of life.'

She stared at him, her mind working fast, 'Bruce, you're inspired!' She had to admit he was right. 'The snag of a holiday like this is the danger of each day becoming a carbon copy of the one before. Something with a bit of adventure is bound to appeal.'

Her blue eyes shone. 'Where exactly is it?' Her voice shook with excitement. Some of the best outings she'd shared with Pip had been on scrambles.

Bruce pulled a map out of an inner pocket and smoothed it out on the small, circular table which separated them, 'Let me see now.' He traced a well-manicured finger across it, and then stabbed at a point near a bridge. 'There—it's a fantastic place—rough and isolated, miles from anywhere. You won't disturb anyone,' he added triumphantly. He unscrewed the top of his Cartier pen and marked the spot with a thick black cross.

Gemma peered down at it and then looked across at him, impressed. 'Terrific,' she admitted generously, rather wishing she'd thought of it herself.

'Oh, I'm trained to come up with new ideas,' he said without false modesty. 'It's all a matter of lateral thinking. You'll soon get the hang of it. And, by the way, it looks just fine to me. I've staked it out. There aren't any walls or hedges. In fact there's nothing at all to indicate it can't be used.'

'It's perfect,' Gemma agreed enthusiastically. She rose to her feet, 'I'll put it to the others.' The faint roar she had detected earlier had became much louder, 'There they are now.'

She wiped her perspiring palms and strolled with as much nonchalance as she could muster into the small bar. She propped herself up on a stool chatting to the wizened barman as she ordered a glass of Somerset cider. Through the window, she saw the jazzily customised bikes crunch over the gravelled courtyard and muffled conversation rose from it. The door swung open and they trooped in noisily. The majority were on holiday in pairs, girl-friends riding pillion, and Gemma, who knew that a ride could be a crucial test for a relationship, felt a sudden surge of responsibility. The rest of the men were on their own and the shy, solo girl rider who had arrived the day before on her Kawasaki had begun to blossom in all the male attention. She had confided to Gemma that she had bought a motor-cycle because she could not afford to drive a car on her waitress's wages. Now she wouldn't be parted from it.

'Great.' A tough-looking biker with a shaven head who had not uttered a syllable since he had checked into the hotel, said unexpectedly. He downed his pint of beer in one gulp. 'Didn't notice all those birds and flowers until I had a read of this.'

He took his well-thumbed hand-out from

his pocket. There were grunts of agreement from the others.

And the rain had not spoilt their day, Gemma heard with relief. It seemed they'd hardly noticed it. Some had gone fishing, others had wandered round churches and through ruined castles and all of them to their astonishment and delight were welcomed in local pubs. They began to swap anecdotes and Gemma felt pleasure wash over her. It was going to work. There was nothing for her to worry about. She caught Bruce's eye and he raised his glass of Dom Perignon to her.

That evening as they tucked into chili con carne Bruce, who had changed into expensive Continental leisure wear, talked about the scramble. They had all settled down well together, united by their love of motor-cycling. They seemed to enjoy his company and took up the suggestion with alacrity. Maps were promptly unrolled and a course plotted.

*   *   *

It was a perfect day, warm with a slight breeze.

'You coming?' the shaven-head biker invited Gemma. She hesitated, but the others noisily took up the plea and she allowed herself to be persuaded. She led the way, Bruce riding pillion in a borrowed helmet. The rest fanned out behind her. It was a good show, she thought proudly as she glanced over her shoulder; a purring Harley-Davidson hobnobbed with a raunchy BMW at low throttle, as a unique self-assembled turbo-charged bike cruised alongside a vintage Vincent Black Lightning.

'Over there,' Bruce gesticulated and they raced onto the site.

Shouting, red-faced, gasping, they twisted down slopes, leapt over a rushing stream, zigzagged through the trees and bumped across deep rabbit holes, their wheels churning up the ground. Their transistors blared above the bellowing exhausts and the fumes hung in the air like poison gas. Bruce as self-appointed referee yelled hoarsely. Gemma energetically joined in and lobbed chocolate to the howling bikers. Then, flaked out, her lungs aching, she withdrew and retreated to the roadside. She leaned breathlessly against the Honda, a sandwich in one hand, her eyes glued to the wheeling mayhem. It was exhilarating. The scramble added the right ingredient to the holiday, the fizz that it needed to make it a resounding success. And she had Bruce to thank for it. The excitement and fresh air made her cheeks glow; she munched contentedly and poured herself coffee from the thermos flask, unaware of an approaching vehicle. The sound of a car door being slammed vigorously made her jump. She swivelled round, spilling coffee down her shirt front. Stefan's face was implacable as he reached her from the Jaguar in two paces.

Just what do you think you're doing?' he grated as he surveyed the scene.

Gemma's heart nearly seemed to stop beating. 'What do you think it looks like? We're enjoying ourselves. Isn't that what it's all about?' she demanded furiously. She couldn't see what it had to do with him. 'Anyway it's none of your business.' Her eyes blazing, she turned back to watch the scramble, her curls tossing in the breeze.

Stefan caught her by the shoulder and twisted her round to face him so that she was only inches away. Anger flared in his face. 'It's very much my business. This is my land and you're trespassing. I was about to call the police but luckily for you I decided to investigate for myself.' His eyes were points of ice. 'And I want you all off it, fast.'

The colour drained from Gemma's face. 'But . . . but . . . it's undefined land on the map. There's nothing to show it's privately owned. We . . . I thought there'd be no problem.' Her voice stuck in her throat.

'Well you're mistaken. You ought to have known better. Surely commonsense dictated that you should have had the wit to make proper enquiries, first? Now just recall your friends before I take this any further.' He raised his voice above the din of the scramble.

Gemma moved slightly and his hand fell away. 'I can't do that,' she stammered. 'I'm very sorry but I need more time, please. Surely you can see we're enjoying ourselves? I can't just call it off and ask them to pack it in. It's just not on. I can't show myself up like this. It'll ruin my business. I'm asking your permission, now. Isn't that good enough for you?' She should have known, Gemma told herself. Instinct should have warned her it was too good to be true. But Stefan couldn't act the grand seigneur now—she'd lose face with the bikers. She shivered involuntarily and forced herself to switch her eyes to his face.

He shook his head. 'I simply can't tolerate this sort of thing on my land. I'm giving you ten minutes to sort it out, then I shall summon the police. This is quite unwarranted.' His green eyes froze.

'What's up, Gem?' Bruce sauntered towards them, jingling the loose change in his pocket.

Gemma introduced them reluctantly, 'It seems this is Stefan's property.' She looked at Stefan anxiously, her eyes pleading. Stefan interjected coolly. 'Not seems. *Is.*'

Bruce turned to Gemma, drawing in his lower lip and explained to her that he had met Stefan at a function in the City some months ago.

'So, as this is yours, you won't mind if we stay?' he remarked breezily. He gave Stefan a disarming smile. 'Will he, Gem?' He slipped a possessive arm round her waist and Gemma stiffened as his thighs lightly brushed hers.

'I mind very much,' Stefan countered, his face a polite mask, 'As I've already told . . . Gem,' he added. His eyes met hers in a cool, level stare and she felt the breath catch in her throat.

'Look here,' Bruce began petulantly, unaccustomed to being thwarted. 'You can't be serious. This is the high point of the week. We can't just up sticks.' He stressed the 'we'. Another wild roar of enthusiasm from the bikers, oblivious to the conflict only yards away, drowned his words. Stefan raised his eyebrows with heavy irony and she glanced away, confused, uncomfortable. Bruce was being very supportive but even she felt he was taking a bit too much on himself.

'You have no choice,' Stefan said with a studied politeness. He started to walk back to the car. Gemma bit her lip and stared frantically at his retreating back—very hard, solid, tapering into loose Japanese style trousers.

'Please—Stefan—wait,' she called desperately.

'Forget it, Gem. What can he possibly do?' Bruce said deprecatingly. He caught her arm but she shook it off, ignoring him. She began to run, stumbling over uneven ground, not caring if it looked undignified. There was more than dignity at stake now. She had to try and salvage things. But she couldn't halt the scramble. It would mean the end of her business venture. Stefan had to be made to see that. The pain of that prospect shot through her and for the first time she realised how much it meant to her, how involved she had become in it.

'Don't go like that,' she cried, 'just listen to me, please.' The furious dash across the gradient of the land combined with her apprehension made her voice sound high and jerky to her. She caught up with Stefan, her heart beating painfully in her chest. Stefan jerked his head in the direction of the car. 'Get in please. I'll deal with Bruce Baxter later,' he warned grimly. He eased himself behind the steering-wheel and turned to face her.

'This has got to stop.'

'I thought it was a wonderful idea, and it still is. They're having a fantastic time. Even you must be able to see that,' she defended herself.

His eyes closed for a moment behind the dark lashes. Suddenly he lifted them, and they were not a hard, cold green, but warm, gentle and questioning. 'But it's wrong,' he said at last. He continued to regard her.

'I wasn't to know that,' she muttered. 'I promise you I thought it was public land. Bruce seemed to . . .' she broke off abruptly lest he thought she was trying to shift the blame. Suddenly she felt very weary—she could take no more of the continual battle of wills that seemed always to surface when they were together.

Stefan sighed and pushed back a lock of her hair which had fallen over her brow. The gesture made her feel curiously vulnerable. His face was so close she could feel his warm breath on her cheek and there was a tiny scar on his brow just below the hairline which she had not noticed before.

His eyes scrutinised her face silently for a moment, then he relented. 'Just this once, then, but you must find another spot for the next time.'

An enormous sense of relief washed over her. Gemma started to thank him, but he cut her short. 'Let this be a lesson to you. You could have ended up with a huge claim for compensation on your hands.'

Dismay prickled her spine. Gemma stared at him, 'I'm not covered for that sort of thing,' she faltered. She lifted a hand to her tumbled hair and he read the consternation in her face.

One dark eyebrow rose lazily. 'Your first two business mistakes,' he pointed out, not unkindly. 'Under-insured and then your failure to find out who owns the land and seek his consent.'

If it had been anyone other than Stefan— the thought made her shiver and she felt very much alone, all too aware how lightly he had let her off.

There was a peremptory knock on the window, 'Open this, please.' Bruce's brow was etched with a frown, 'Are you giving her a hard time, Radulescu? I demand to know what's going on. Gem, let me deal with this.' He rattled his knuckles against the bodywork.

Gemma turned to Stefan, 'Shouldn't I . . .' she began tentatively. 'Oh . . .', she gasped as he slipped the Jaguar into gear. It glided rapidly and soundlessly away. Bruce stared after it, a shout dying on his lips.

'Where are you going?' Gemma was torn between sympathy for Bruce and her relief at Stefan's willingness to overlook her stupidity.

'Somewhere fools like Baxter definitely can't rush in.' His voice was suddenly very harsh.

'Isn't that a little unfair?' Gemma protested, 'Bruce's help was given in good faith.'

Stefan smiled rather grimly, 'Your confidence in him is touching if somewhat misplaced. If you haven't grasped that yet, you're more naïve than I thought.' The car sped smoothly along the winding coastal road, and she caught a glimpse of the steely grey North Sea as they began to climb.

Gemma bit back a sharp retort. 'You've got the wrong impression of him,' she pointed out reasonably.

The broad shoulders shrugged, 'Well, well, he's cannier than I gave him credit for.' He braked gently to let a flock of sheep cross the road to the field on the opposite side.

'This is becoming ridiculous,' Gemma thought. 'I'm not sure what I'm supposed to

88

make of that.' She deliberately lightened her tone, and stared out of the window to admire the majestic ruins of a castle stolid on the hillside.

'You will, in time,' his voice was even, unemotional as if he had tired of the subject and considered it closed. Gemma glanced back and found him looking at her with an unreadable expression on his face.

Gemma felt uncomfortable and laced her fingers together. How totally different Stefan and Bruce were. It was probably the clash of personality which prompted the antipathy between them. Stefan was bound to feel hostile towards him after what had occurred that day. But Bruce was wise enough to want to make his peace with him and it would all blow over. The prospect of that made her feel more relaxed, easier. But equally she couldn't afford any more confrontations with her trustee—even Bruce would have the sense to realise that.

She glanced at him again and her heart began to hammer as the green eyes held hers intently. But she noticed that the tension had eased from his face, lean brown fingers lightly on the steering-wheel. She had a sudden image of his hands on her body caressing it into a climax of love and she went weak with longing. She lowered her eyes quickly, confused, colour staining her cheeks.

'Hell of a coincidence meeting Baxter here,'

he commented drily. His eyes were keen.

Gemma groaned inwardly. He wasn't going to let her escape as easily from this one. But she was equally resolute. She had no intention of providing Stefan with a long-winded explanation. It was really none of his business.

'He signed on for a holiday.' It was not entirely untrue, Gemma told herself, hoping Stefan would leave it at that. His mouth twitched and his eyebrows raised fractionally. Gemma stared out of the window to avoid his steady gaze.

'I'd have thought he'd feel more at home on the French Riviera,' he persisted pleasantly.

Gemma forced a vague note into her voice. 'Oh, I don't know him well enough to vouch for his likes and dislikes. But there must have been something about Speedwell Holidays that appealed to him, otherwise he'd hardly have come. It's rather an acquired taste, don't you think?' She threw the ball back at him.

He caught it swiftly, 'Easily acquired I should have thought when there is so much to gain.'

Gemma looked puzzled, 'I don't know what you mean. Bruce isn't getting a free holiday. He can afford this sort of thing, ten times over. In fact, I'm the one who's gained from the exciting new ideas for the business he's managed to come up with,' she flashed back.

'Like the scramble, you mean?' he reminded her pointedly. 'That was a potential liability.

What other crazy schemes are you collaborating with him on?' His tone was terse, the words bitten off. 'Come on, I'm waiting.'

'Nothing positive, yet,' she conceded unwillingly, judging from the lines of impatience round his mouth that his temper was wearing thin. 'But we're working on it,' she added with a touch of defiance.

He slowed down as they approached a centuries-old stone bridge.

'King James VI of Scotland galloped hot-foot over this down to England to claim *his* inheritance.' He glanced at her and continued:

'May I remind you of the terms of the trust. Your efforts and yours alone. No one else is allowed to aid and abet you,' he insisted.

'So I'll have to do without Pip?' Gemma felt as if she was drowning. He couldn't expect her to do everything single handed. Pip's part time help with the office chores was invaluable. But even more indispensable was her moral support. 'I can't do that,' she looked at him in stunned incredulity.

His voice broke in on her thoughts. 'Pip's services are essential. Baxter's are not. He's caused you enough problems already. Is that understood?' Stefan's tone was charged with steel.

Gemma took a deep breath to steady herself. 'OK. Business-wise I'm on my own.' It was a qualified assent and the only one Stefan was entitled to ask for. She could not let him dictate to her, her choice of friends.

He put out a hand and lifted her chin gently, his fingers cool, his eyes as green as emeralds. 'I know you're a woman of your word.' As he touched her, something deep in her tightened and her lashes fluttered involuntarily against her cheeks.

The rest of the journey continued in silence, but it was companionable. Gemma stared out of the window as the XJ6 sped silently through the rolling border countryside, the sky above it an endless, brilliant blue. Save for the occasional passing vehicle, it was vast and awesomely empty. Presently Stefan swung off the main road through tall, wrought-iron gates and halted at the end of a short, red-gravelled drive.

'Here we are.' The house was large, its Georgian exterior carefully restored. The rough stone weathered by years of rain and mist had reduced the surface to a smoothness that shone like pale corn in the sunlight. Stefan got out of the car. Gemma hesitated then, more slowly, followed him up a short flight of stone steps. As if on cue, the front door opened. A short, tubby man in a black suit smiled and bowed slightly to her as he spoke to Stefan in a language which she did not recognise. Then she remembered what Pip had said. Of course, it must be Romanian. It had a beautiful sound, expressive and melodic, instantly conjuring up a mental picture of serenading gypsy violins in a sun-dappled garden restaurant.

'My butler Pavel. He and his wife Marianne housekeep for me.' Stefan introduced them briskly, as he motioned to her to precede him into the house, lightly placing his hand on her shoulder. His touch almost scorched her and she hurried through before him, her heart pounding suddenly. The large square entrance hall was not what she expected. Gemma fought down a gasp of surprise. It was in marked contrast with Stefan's sophisticated Eaton Square apartment to which she had paid a flying visit a few weeks before to sign some legal documents. But his country home threw a completely different slant on the man. There was a homely clutter in the hall—it was strewn with trophies of an active, outdoor life. Mounted high on one wall was a pair of stag's antlers and a collection of fishing-rods stood in one corner. Sundry country-life magazines lay scattered on an octagonal maplewood table across which a flat tweed cap had been carelessly tossed.

Stefan led the way into the drawing-room. Facing her as she entered was a magnificent icon of the Virgin Mary. The saint's face held an expression of such sadness, that Gemma felt very close to tears. Almost mesmerised by the intense beauty of the object, she stood silently in front of it for a few moments. It was not something she had thought Stefan would possess. It seemed too devotional to be regarded simply as another work of art. Stefan was only inches from her and she was all too aware of the strong muscles beneath his black tee-shirt and the leanness of his hips. A pulse began to beat in her neck.

'A symbol of perfect womanhood, don't you think? It was left to me by my grandmother,' he said softly. 'After the abdication of King Michael of Romania, during the last war, many Romanians fled the country. Some, like my grandparents, settled in England. That's how my parents met. Both sets of families had known each other well in Bucharest so it was natural that they should gravitate together in a foreign country.'

Gemma nodded. She looked round the large room. Apart from the icon, the curiously impersonal feel about it was striking, unlike the sudden intimacy of the front hall.

'Now, you're not on your bike now. Can I offer you a drink?' He moved towards a trolley laden with a variety of bottles.

Gemma checked the time, and registered with a shock that it was well past six o'clock. 'Not sherry,' she replied promptly. Men always assumed that women would plump for sherry, and Stefan, whose hand had strayed to the decanter of dry fino, paused. He raised his eyebrows, 'Name your poison, then.' He grinned wickedly at her over his shoulder.

'Vodka and tonic,' Gemma didn't hesitate.

It was her favourite and brought back a remembered remark of Uncle Arthur that it was a sneaky tipple since its smell was indiscernible on the breath.

'A sophisticated drink,' he observed, pouring out a generous measure.

'I'm a sophisticated woman,' Gemma watched him top up the chunky glass with tonic water. Something in his tone made her feel suddenly furious.

'Now that's very interesting.' Stefan handed her her drink and took a sip of his own—rare, malt whisky. He looked at her directly with an odd expression on his face as he registered the fury beginning to glitter in her eyes.

'Interesting?' she repeated, outraged. 'That's a very convenient way of putting it. What exactly do you mean by that?'

He leaned nonchalantly against the pink-veined marble mantelpiece. 'It means what it says. Nothing more or less,' his voice was amused, his eyes teasing.

'Don't patronise me,' Gemma snapped, sitting upright in the soft, cream silk sofa in which she had been lolling moments earlier. 'All right. I'll tell you what it means, or rather what it doesn't. It's one of those bland, colourless phrases that really don't mean anything . . .' she stopped, her skin stinging with hot colour.

'Now we're getting somewhere.' He sat down at the opposite end of the sofa, 'so that's it. You chink I'm rather bland.' Panic suddenly hit her as Gemma began to feel she was walking into a well-sprung trap.

'I didn't say that,' a denial rose to her lips.

'What did you say then?' his eyes darkened, changed. Gemma tensed, fighting the sensations he had aroused in her. Every nerve ending in her body felt raw with longing. Could she honestly tell him that he was the most infuriating, dangerous man she had ever met? No. If you wanted to preserve any shred of self-identity, you did not tell a man like Stefan that you did not know what to make of him or that he confused you. That would hardly be sophisticated.

'Perhaps I just expressed myself rather badly,' she said shakily, disturbed by her thoughts. She forced herself to appear cool and normal.

He looked at her intently for one long moment and Gemma could feel her heart beating over-rate.

*　　　*　　　*

'Let me show you blandness in reverse,' Stefan said, very softly. An arm encircled her shoulders and she could hear his sharpened breathing.

'I . . .' her words were smothered by the pressure of his mouth, insistent, deepening, parting her lips, his tongue a sensuous

96

marauder as he slid one hand along the nape of her neck caressing the smooth skin below her hair. Her whole body felt heavy, drugged, his physical contact with her slow, deliberate, almost melting her bones. His breath touched her cheeks as he tightened his hold, his other hand slipping down to cup a breast. A harsh cry of need escaped her, as desire flooded through her. She closed her eyes tightly as his body pressed against her, as his mouth caught hers, roughly, urgently. Instinctively, her fingers reached up to the thickness of his dark hair, her body arching against him.

'Gemma, I've been wanting to say—' He lifted his head and a tremor passed through her as he set her free abruptly. He rose to his feet and drew the heavy, swagged curtains across the window. Gemma made a superhuman effort to match his assurance, but the physical hunger was still acute. She found herself shaking. He slanted her an all-seeing glance as though he fathomed her unspoken need instinctively. He snapped on the table lamp and the light burst into a warm glow under the red silk shade. Gradually she recovered her composure. 'What I find rather odd,' Gemma observed coolly, forcing her voice to sound unflustered, 'is the sort of unfinished look about this room.'

'Unfinished?' he laughed quietly. 'It isn't even started.'

'Why's that?' she asked, trying to still her

97

fluttering pulse beat.

'My wife will have to sort out all that.' His back was towards her, his buttocks hard, muscled.

Steel bands clutched at her chest. 'Your wife . . . I . . . wasn't aware you were married.' Her voice caught low in her throat.

Stefan swung round to face her. 'Neither was I! But one day I will and she will have *carte blanche* with the decorations.' He sounded casual but his eyes raked hers unmercifully. A woman of sophistication would nod, ask if he had someone specific in mind, Gemma reminded herself. What was the classic question? To her surprise, she asked it.

'Do I know her?' It came calmly, tinged almost with disinterest.

He gave her a quick look and she returned it, her heart still hammering.

He thrust his thumbs inside his trouser tops and drawled. 'I hope one day you'll know her as well as you know yourself.' It was the sort of unsettling remark he was master of.

Gemma curled up in the sofa, her shapely legs folded under her, 'One day?' she arched all enquiring brow, 'that sounds very much in the future. Why not soon?' Suddenly she felt an irresistible urge to lose no time in meeting the woman in his life.

'Some day soon, then,' he said with mock gravity, giving nothing away. They burst out laughing, lightening the charged atmosphere.

There was a soft knock on the door and Pavel entered. He exchanged a few words with Stefan in Romanian. Pavel looked expectantly at her.

'I'm sure you can guess what he said. Of course, you'll stay to supper.'

He crooked his arm formally and Gemma slipped hers through it self-consciously, as he escorted her into the dining-room. The table was covered with a richly embroidered peasant-style cloth and laid with naïvely decorated pottery dishes.

Everything about the meal was linked with a Romanian theme. The food, the wine, the music that played softly on the compact disc. It was obvious to her that Stefan had not abandoned his heritage. She listened fascinated as he talked of holidays spent frequently in the homeland of his parents and grandparents—of the wildfowl in the marshes of the Danube and the forests of the Delta, fishing in the snow-fed streams and hunting the brown bear. And Gemma, whose knowledge of that country nestling in south-eastern Europe was limited to plum jam, fiery tennis players and Dracula, was transported to another world, and only longed to hear more.

CHAPTER FOUR

Several days had elapsed since the near calamitous scramble. A completely new party of bikers had arrived since then but Bruce showed no obvious signs of departing although he kept reminding Gemma, rather self-importantly she thought, that he had a string of deals awaiting his attention. 'We're fully booked,' reported Pip gleefully over the telephone. She and Gemma kept in touch on a daily basis to enable Gemma to keep track of the paperwork. 'The upward curve shows no sign of dropping off. In fact I've had so many enquiries that I've had to open a reserve list, just in case we get any cancellations—they're that keen.'

'That's just what I wanted to hear,' Gemma said enthusiastically. 'We're certainly not doing too badly.'

'You mean you aren't,' corrected Pip, simply. 'It was your brain-child and it's certainly paying off. Now take credit where credit's due.'

'But I couldn't have managed without you,' Gemma pointed out truthfully. A warm glow of satisfaction crept through her. Pip was right. If it turned out to be a success story, she was the mastermind behind it. It would have been all her doing. Gemma studied the computer spread-sheet which Pip regularly sent to her. The figures spoke for themselves—there would be no need to fudge anything when it came to the final balance sheet. Speedwell Holidays was on its way to making a profit. No, Gemma corrected the self-effacing understatement; not a modest but a distinctly handsome profit.

She sucked in her cheeks thoughtfully. The scramble had been voted a great hit, but that had been one of Bruce's ideas. She had to invent some innovative schemes of her own if he wasn't to get a stranglehold on her little business empire. She couldn't help recalling the conversation she'd had with him after that unexpected Romanian dinner with Stefan.

'You came in rather late last night,' Bruce sounded reproachful as he eyed her narrowly over the breakfast table.

Gemma finished spreading thick chunky marmalade on a piece of toast before answering. 'I wasn't aware I was accountable to you.' A broad smile robbed the retort of offence.

Bruce looked taken aback and she noticed that his ears went suddenly crimson.

'Just an observation, Gem,' he recovered himself quickly, 'but honestly, I was so worried I was thinking of organising a search-party.' He screwed up his face to demonstrate his concern but the anxiety-stricken look didn't quite come off, Gemma thought, giggling to herself. 'Incidentally, did you manage to mollify Radulescu? We can't afford to have him harbouring a grudge against us. He could prove a dangerous adversary and that's the last thing our budding business needs.'

'My business, you mean, surely?' Gemma corrected him quickly. She fastened him with a look which she hoped would serve as a warning to him to keep his predatory hands off Speedwell. 'My business,' she repeated firmly and more loudly as if to emphasise the point, 'and I want to keep it that way. Of course, all ideas are welcome but I'm going to decide if I want to use them and when and how.'

Bruce's voice took on an injured tone, 'Well, that's a U-turn, if ever there was one. Only a few days ago you practically appointed me as your business consultant. Come on now—even you've got to admit I've come up with some tremendously popular ideas.'

'I appointed you, what?' Was there no limit to the impertinence of the man? Had he really no idea what he had cost her? She was not going to let him get away with that. 'Your ideas were so fantastic they could have got me into trouble—serious trouble. If Stefan hadn't been so amenable and prepared to overlook your bungling, I could have been facing one helluva claim for compensation.' Suppressed anger made her hands shake and she had to clasp them together tightly in her lap.

Bruce had regained his composure and

seemed to be quite unflustered by her sudden outburst. He probably thrived on confrontations, she thought wryly. He was the sort of man who would manufacture a confrontation if there was none in reality, just to get his adrenalin going.

He leaned over and patted her arm. 'Calm down, Gem, I promise not to get you into any more trouble. *Pax*? Now we *are* still friends, arena we? If you want to invest any profits from your business, or from any other source . . .' he paused significantly, 'just let we know. I have the very thing for you. A flourishing offshore investment scheme where the yield is extremely high and the income is all tax free. You couldn't find anything more competitive if you tried.' He eyed her expectantly.

Gemma sighed deeply. That was Bruce all over, she thought wearily. Impervious to the havoc he caused. But then an inner voice reminded her, he couldn't be blamed exclusively. She had been a willing, if foolish, collaborator borne away by his infectious enthusiasm. Well, she had certainly learned her lesson.

Gemma smiled at him, a little ashamed of herself. 'You're incorrigible!'

Bruce grinned back like a naughty boy. 'Ah but immensely lovable—I hope.' He back-tracked. 'So Stefan's your trustee. There must be a crock of gold stashed away somewhere otherwise I couldn't see someone as high and

103

mighty as Radulescu bothering himself with peanuts.'

Gemma cleared her throat, feeling a little stunned. 'I don't know,' she deliberately sounded vague, 'Uncle Arthur and Stefan were friends. That's how it all came about. A last favour for an old buddy.'

Surely Bruce didn't know what was really at stake? Gemma was certain that Pip would never breach a confidence. Yet Pip might have unwittingly said something to her brother Richard who in turn could have carelessly blurted it out to Bruce. People like Bruce made it their business to probe, to dig for the ins and outs.

He studied her face thoughtfully, 'But . . . oh well, not to worry . . .' he checked himself and flicked a bread crumb off his trousers, 'So what are your plans for today?'

*   *   *

'So what are your plans for today?' Bruce's familiar catch-phrase rang loudly in Gemma's ears bringing her abruptly back to the present. She looked up to see him standing in front of her in immaculate French leisure wear. The sun shone from a cloudless blue sky and it felt as if it was going to be a hot day. Gemma wore a sleeveless pink and white striped dress, her bare arms soft and smooth. Bruce's glance strayed appreciatively over her, lingering on the waist clinching belt. She donned her large white-rimmed sunglasses, 'What do you know about Lindisfarne?' she asked.

Bruce pulled out a chair. 'That's one of those small islands just off the coast, isn't it? Known for its seals and birds, the feathered variety, I mean.' He couldn't resist chortling at the feeble joke and cocked his head at her.

Gemma prompted him 'And . . . ?'

'I'm stumped. Is there anything else?'

Gemma sprang to her feet. 'It's also called Holy Island. Saint Aidan and his community of monks settled there and illustrated the Lindisfarne Gospels. Exquisite and . . . priceless.' She shot a sly look at Bruce, 'I thought you'd know . . . expert as you are on items of value . . .' She couldn't resist the dig. 'It has a marvellous castle refurbished by Lutyens at the top of a volcanic crag. It'll make a super excursion for a day out. I'm going to reconnoitre.'

Her excitement was infectious and Bruce succumbed immediately, looking interested. 'Great Gem, just great. Look, why don't we get over there in the car? It'll be so much more comfortable and to be frank this biking lark's not my scene. I promise to let you potter around on your own, then we can join up for a spot of lunch there and make a day of it.'

Gemma rubbed her cheek with the tip of her finger. It sounded an excellent idea. What with Bruce doing the driving, she could focus her concentration on absorbing all the local colour that was likely to whet the bikers' appetites. 'Done,' she agreed enthusiastically.

Soon they were on the open road, the hood of the Porsche pulled well back, sunshine and fresh air streaming through the open-topped car.

'I've checked the times of the tides,' Bruce reassured her as he put his foot down on the accelerator and overtook a car pulling a caravan. There was a car coming towards them and he had to brake suddenly to avoid it.

Gemma had completely forgotten about that. 'Well done,' she sounded impressed. It was silly of her to have forgotten such a vital detail. When the tide was out, vehicles could cross from the mainland at the narrowest point via the causeway which was separated from it by a wide area of mud flats and salt marsh. But at high tide the only way to get across to Holy Island was by boat and the mud flats were littered with salt-ruined car wrecks whose owners had failed to check the tide tables. They had not motored very far when Bruce suddenly struck his forehead with the palm of his hand and pulled up outside a telephone booth. He rummaged in his pocket for a phone card. 'Won't be a tic,' he said as he opened the car door, 'I just want to check on some things back at the office.' Gemma watched him go, his bulging black leather filofax in one hand.

He was back sooner than she expected, his

thin lips pressed firmly together. He got in and slammed the car door with what seemed to her to be unwarranted force.

'Anything wrong?' Gemma sensed that something was amiss.

'Wrong?' His mouth twisted and he gave a harsh, hollow laugh that made her suddenly shiver with unease. 'That's an understatement. I can't go into it now. I'll have to get back to the hotel and make some more phone calls. Something's blown up.'

'But.' Gemma started dismayed, 'What about Holy Island?' Indignation showed in her eyes. Damn Bruce, she thought unsympathetically. He thought nothing of letting people down and wriggling out of a prior arrangement when it suited him.

'Don't say it, I know. You don't have to rub it in,' he conceded irritably as he revved the engine. 'I'll run you there, but I can't stay. You'll be able to find your own way back. There're plenty of coaches and buses there this time of year. Pity about lunch.' It was the only thing he sounded genuinely regretful about, Gemma thought furiously. Well, she consoled herself. At least she'd get a one-way lift. It was the least he could do. Bruce said very little for the rest of the journey, his shoulders set in a sullen hunch as the car sped dangerously along the winding coast road, consistently exceeding the speed limit.

Soon they were passing over the causeway, a

narrow strip of metalled tarmac bordered by damp, sandy soil on either side.

The poles which once guided pilgrims across to the priory still existed, she noticed. Once onto the island, Bruce pulled up with a flourish in the road opposite the imposing statue of St. Aidan. 'Here you are. See you at dinner. Too bad about all this, but business beckons. Here,' he thrust a scrap of paper into her hand, 'I jotted down the times of the safe crossings.' He barely gave her a chance to decant herself before he was turning the car round in the road.

Gemma waved, personally pleased to be on her own. She could take as long as she liked over her soundings of the tiny islet without feeling guilty about it. It would be an exploration of sacred ground where the monks and saints of old had trod the earth in the sixth century in their task to convert the heathens of the mainland. The ruined priory conjured up the past in an immediate and vivid fashion— the splendour of the soaring priory roof—the monks' parlour, the kitchen. Gemma noticed with amusement that the Father Abbot had elected to have his cell closest to the kitchen, to derive the full benefit of the warmth emanating from it.

Afterwards Gemma walked carefully up the steep ramp approach to the castle perched on the hill. There was no rope or rail to clutch as she trod the herring-bone pattern of cobble stones. She could see only too easily how such splendour had captured the imagination of Hudson, the owner of a magazine company, at the turn of the century.

Together with his architect friend Edwin Lutyens, a rising young star in the architectural firmament, they rebuilt the castle and created an interior which was both austere and comfortable, the sombre Dutch pictures and the solid oak furniture softened by the gleam of polished copper. The view from it was stunning. It must have been a wonderful refuge from the cares of everyday life, Gemma thought. She caught a glimpse of Bamburgh Castle and below, quite clearly, the priory ruins and out at sea, the Farne Islands. It was an evocative place—an island of romance and magic.

Gemma filled page after page in her notebook with her impressions, convinced that the bikers would enjoy it as much as she had. There were tea-rooms in whitewashed cottages, pubs and souvenir shops. She wandered down to one such now and ordered a snack for herself It was a typically Northumbrian dish—Craster kippers with thickly buttered brown bread accompanied by a pot of strong tea. Gemma ate quickly, and realised she had had nothing since breakfast. She knew she'd never have been able to persuade Bruce to sample any such regional dish. He would have insisted on *haute cuisine* impressively presented in a stylish restaurant on the mainland. But Gemma was convinced that this was the sort of food, wholesome and filling, that would appeal to the bikers, with appetites made all the more keen by the bracing sea air.

The sky which had been cloudless when she had started out had become overcast and, even as she emerged from the cafe, the drizzle had begun to turn to a downpour. Gemma groaned, rubbing her goose-pimpled arms. Why hadn't she had the foresight to have brought a jacket or a light mac with her? 'I'll be soaked through by the time I get to the main road,' Gemma thought grimly as, head down, she ran through the village to the causeway. There didn't appear to be any coaches and buses about, she thought. That was strange, considering the number of people she had seen earlier on the island that day. Someone shouted something unintelligible to her and waved both hands. Gemma returned the greeting but did not stop. He shouted and gestured again but this time Gemma didn't reciprocate. He couldn't have chosen a less opportune moment to try and chat her up, she thought irritably.

It was bucketing down. The breeze had backed to a stiff, cruel wind. Perhaps that accounted for the depth of briny water on the causeway. It was ankle deep and rising fast by each passing minute. Gemma bent down and unstrapped her sandals, holding them in one hand. The causeway was curiously deserted she noticed as she plodded slowly across it. The next thing she knew she had lost her footing and slipped. Excruciating pain shot up through her right ankle as she collapsed in a heap. Even the slightest movement served only to exacerbate the pain. She was drenched, her legs and dress bespattered by damp mud and the level of the seawater continued its inexorable rise. 'This can't just be the heavy rain,' Gemma thought worriedly as she rose slowly and hobbled across trying to keep the weight off her injured ankle. Then it occurred to her—it could only mean one thing. The tide was coming in and coming in at a ferocious speed.

She glanced at her watch and checked the tide tables on the screwed up ball of scrap paper in her pocket. They did not tally. The jumbled mass of figures in green biro looked more like stock exchange prices to her than a time table. Bruce had bungled it again. Fear clutched at her, making her stomach knot with tension. She was all alone. No-one would miss her. She was not expected back by Bruce until much later. He would not worry if he did not catch her that evening. He would assume that she had decided to stay on the island overnight. And by the morning, it would have been too late. She'd have been drowned and washed out to sea. Her body wouldn't be recovered for months.

Gemma felt as if she had come to the end of everything. She could almost see the few lines tucked insignificantly away in a spare slot on the sports page of the local paper. 'Mystery body found by fisherman. Believed to be that of Gemma Wells reported missing last Summer.' Gemma forced herself to block out the morbid thoughts that assailed her and hobbled grimly on. The sea-level was now calf high and bits of driftwood and seaweed swirled about her legs, clinging limpet-like to them. Gemma tucked the end of her dress into the top of her knicker elastic. Her ankle throbbed unbearably and she stopped, wincing in agony. Feeling utterly wretched, she surveyed the causeway.

There was still a good deal of it to negotiate before she was on dry land. And she could hardly retrace her steps to Holy Island, either. She'd never make it back there with her injured ankle. She wondered how far she was from the little wooden safety hut which she'd barely registered, whilst driven at high speed by Bruce. She screwed up her eyes and scanned the causeway willing the small tower to rise of its own accord out of the gloom. Was that it? Or was it just a mirage which stranded desert travellers see? Was that her lifeline at last or just a trick of her addled brain? There was only one way of finding out. Gemma inched her way forward, pain shearing through her.

Gradually the faint outline took on the sharpness of reality. Tears of relief pierced the back of her eyelids. She reached out and clung thankfully to the stilts that propped it up. There were several wooden steps leading from the sea-level to the safety of the single windowed tower. The sea swirled angrily about her making the hut rock dangerously. Gemma gritted her teeth and hauled herself up step by step, falling at last onto the floor of the hut with a sense of deliverance.

She wiped her tear-stained face with the back of a hand. The rain had stopped but not the unceasing, inexorable inevitability of the in-coming tide. She could feel the raw dank air in her lungs. Darkness had fallen. It was a starless evening, but a faint light glimmered from the cottages on the island. They seemed so near now that she had found a haven that the situation seemed suddenly very ridiculous. That she should be marooned up here, stuck in a hut in the middle of the sea when folk, only a mile away, sat in front of their television sets, cocooned in their homes. But it was obvious she would have to stay here until the tide turned. That could be several hours at least. Gemma gently fingered her ankle. It had swollen and continued to ache at the slightest movement. She prayed it wasn't broken. That would be absolutely devastating to say the least, during what looked like being

Speedwell's busiest weeks.

As the sea surged round the hut making the window pane rattle, Gemma's fears, temporarily allayed by the safe haven she had reached, returned anew. Suppose it collapsed or a freak wave submerged it? It would be hours before the tide receded to a level that was safe enough to enable her to continue her journey to the mainland. Gemma changed her position on the floor of the look-out. It was hard and cold. Her body ached all over. She felt as if it would never recover from such a battering. For the umpteenth time she wondered how Bruce could have been so crassly negligent. A faint throbbing sounded from a distance. Yes, there it was again, she could hear it quite distinctly above the roar of the sea. Gemma crawled on her knees to the opposite side of the look-out and straightened up slowly, leaning for support against the wall. Coming towards the hut was a small motorboat; through the misted up window she could see its lights blazing. Gemma rummaged in her bag for a hanky and waved the speck of white but without much real hope that it would be spotted.

The boat was coming nearer and nearer, its engine now a steady drone, riding the waves effortlessly like a dart flying through the air. Please God, let it see me, Gemma prayed. She shook her hanky frantically—it seemed pitifully small to attract any attention, she thought wildly.

'Help, help—over here!' Gemma shouted hoarsely. For a moment it looked as if it would thunder past, oblivious to her ordeal. The disappointment was so keen that she felt as if she wanted to just lie down and die. But no. It had spotted her, or rather spotted something which bore further investigation. It slowed down, turned round and edged itself towards the hut. Gemma could see it now—its name in silver letters painted along its royal blue bow. *Lady Luck.* Gemma let out an unembarrassed whoop of joy. She could hardly believe it, when she'd almost given up hope. The boat bobbed up and down. 'Ahoy there!' The calm, deep voice was unmistakable. Stefan adroitly manoeuvred the boat alongside.

'Am I glad to see you,' Gemma called back, her voice cracking with relief 'My ankle's playing up, though.'

'Stay right there. I'll have you aboard in no time.' *Lady Luck* swayed nearer and nearer.

'That's as near as I can take her,' his voice sounded immensely comforting. 'Now jump.'

Gemma gasped. She glanced down at what seemed a vast expanse of blackness between the hut and the boat.

'I can't . . .'

'You must and you will.' Stefan ordered calmly and from the lights on board she could see his face was set in concentration. 'Come on—one, two, and over!'

At the sound of the last syllable, Gemma shut her eyes tightly and leapt. She landed on his chest, between his arms, panting as much from a sense of having been reprieved as from fear, her cheek becalmed against the soft material of his shirt. The relief at rescue was so immense that she could scarcely drag herself away from the safety of those strong arms, that solid body.

Then she felt his fingers on her hair, pulling her head back, forcing her to look at him and thrusting her body towards him so that his thighs brushed hers. 'What the hell were you trying to prove? I thought I'd lost—' he checked himself. The boat bobbed up and down and he continued to grip her lest she lost her balance and fell.

'Put this on.' He tossed over his orange windcheater and then let her go as he swung the boat away from the hut, the noise of the engine mercifully giving her time to catch her breath and think of a suitable rebuttal. Now that she'd been rescued her innate fighting spirit which had so cruelly deserted her, returned.

'I wasn't trying to prove anything,' she shot back. 'I just got caught unawares,' she added plaintively.

Stefan gave a dismissive snort. 'Well you're damned lucky you made it to the hut.'

'How did you know where to find me?' Gemma began to squeeze the water from her hair.

Stefan paused briefly, 'Baxter,' he said laconically.

'Bruce! How—what do you mean?' Gemma's astonishment was genuine.

'When you didn't show up for supper at the hotel, Baxter started to get worried. I dropped by to deliver the crash helmet you'd left behind at my house the other night and ran into him, propping up the bar. He was in a fair state despite his laid-back exterior. Started to beat his breast and became quite maudlin. Agonising over the fact that he'd unintentionally given you a lot of misleading information, I didn't wait to hear anymore. I boarded *Lady Luck*, and hoped you'd had the sense to anchor at the hut.'

She thought she caught a caressing look in his green eyes but told herself she must have imagined it. 'Thank you, Sir Galahad,' Gemma murmured. She could not cloak her relief at rescue. 'But I suppose you could say I contributed to this sorry state of affairs. The causeway was already pretty well under water when I started across it. I should have realised what had happened.'

'I'd like to tan Baxter's hide,' Stefan muttered grimly, a line between his brows. Gemma saw his lips thin and tighten and realised that he meant it, and would have done it, if this had been another century.

'He's quite the most irresponsible person

I've ever met. A bloody walking disaster. Everything he gets involved in he taints. If anything had happened to—' he stopped himself.

Gemma wondered if Stefan was somehow by inference including her in his derogatory remarks. She said nothing, feeling that it was not the moment to protest. If it hadn't been for Stefan she'd still have been marooned in the hut, getting more panic-stricken with the passing minutes.

Lady Luck glided over the waves and soon they had reached the shore.

Stefan sprang off first and made the boat fast. Then he stretched out his lean body and grasped her by the hand. 'Get moving,' he shouted. It was only a short distance between the boat and the jetty and she could have done it unaided but for some unaccountable reason she clung to his hand and was curiously reluctant to let it go. Once ashore, he hurried her to his Volvo. He switched on the car heater. Her hair began to dry and her garments began to feel less damp. In the comfort of the upholstered seats and the warmth of the car, she began to feel more cheerful.

'I'm driving you back to the hotel—you'll want to change out of those,' he said unnecessarily.

Gemma grimaced and shot him a glance front under lowered eyelashes. 'Why is it that I always seem to encounter you when I'm sodden, damp and in inextricably life-threatening situations?'

Stefan chuckled unexpectedly, 'I was beginning to wonder myself. You must have a penchant for living dangerously.'

'Living dangerously and dying ignominiously,' Gemma said, suddenly very sombre. First a narrow escape from the ravages of the hurricane and then this sea rescue. She could do without any more dramas. She'd had enough to last a lifetime.

Stefan slackened speed as the car approached the hotel, crunching slowly up the gravelled drive. Gemma shot him a fleeting glance and drew an inward sigh of relief. Although his profile was still stern, he had lost that withering look which earlier had made her flinch.

At the sound of the car's wheels on the gravel, Gemma saw Bruce run out of the front entrance, his face as white as chalk. An enormous smile crossed his face when he saw her in the front passenger seat. He grasped the door handle and pulled it open even before the car had halted completely.

'If anything had happened to you, I'd have . . .' Bruce muttered hoarsely. It sounded so different coming from him, Gemma thought wryly. 'But let's not dwell on what happened. You're safe and sound and that's all that matters. Come on in,' he urged as she alighted gingerly from Stefan's car. 'I bet you could do with a stiff brandy. Oh, I say,' he turned almost as an afterthought to Stefan who had watched him without a word, 'thanks—joining us for a drink?'

Stefan was beside Bruce in two ticks. A muscle twitched in his jaw and for one moment, Gemma saw white rage at the surface, checked from exploding over by an almost superhuman effort of will. Stefan stared at Bruce, now restored to his smooth, unruffled self, for a long moment heavy with foreboding. Bruce gave a sudden grin, Gemma noticed with trepidation, quite oblivious to the havoc he had wreaked. Without another word, Stefan strode quickly into the building. Bruce shrugged with bewilderment and did not seem to notice when Gemma withdrew her arm from his when he had earlier linked it with his own.

Stefan had already ordered a round, and it was there, waiting on a small table. He cradled his glass of whisky in his hand. Gemma sipped at the balloon glass of brandy and Bruce made quick work of the gin and tonic, ordering himself a refresher.

'So, sound in wind and limb, then Gem?' Bruce asked breezily and raised his glass to her. 'Here's to a happy return.'

Gemma murmured something incomprehensible under her breath and shifted uneasily in her chair. Bruce was blind to the fact that it was he who was responsible for her dilemma.

'You're a bloody liability, Baxter,' Stefan cut across, cold, controlled, but the fury behind it was unmistakable.

Gemma shivered.

'You could have got the woman drowned with your crass stupidity.'

Bruce gazed at him in a glazed manner and Gemma realised that he must have been drinking steadily since Stefan had last seen him.

'Waszat you said?' he leaned forward, his speech now very slurred. He placed a hand on Gemma's knee and she moved away.

Stefan looked at him contemptuously and continued his inexorable denunciation. 'You landed her in it. You practically killed her. If you weren't so stupid and drunk, I'd hit you for a six.' His voice was low, the tone hard, savage.

Bruce shook his head and grinned vacantly. He wagged his index finger at his inquisitor, 'Not my fault, ol' boy,' he denied solemnly. 'She could have checked the times of the crossings. They're displayed on large public notices plastered all over the island. You can't miss 'em.' He leaned back in his chair, satisfied and hiccuped.

Stefan gave him a disdainful glance. He was determined to tear Bruce off a strip. 'There was no reason why she should check. She had, or thought she had, all the info. she needed to get safely home. She wasn't to know you'd made a balls-up. How could she?'

Gemma saw that Bruce had gone beyond the point when no amount of accusations would have an impact on him. He burped noisily and slumped in his seat. His face began to take on a greenish tinge, she thought, alarmed. Stefan saw it coming, too.

'Oh Lord, not this,' Stefan groaned, 'Let's get him out of here before he disgraces himself and us all.' He swivelled round and signalled a biker from a small party who was looking on interestedly. With the help of the well-built punk—he was a bouncer in a club, Gemma later learnt, Stefan got Bruce up to his room in the nick of time before he threw up violently.

'I've left him to sleep it off,' Stefan announced to her half an hour later. He made no attempt to conceal a smile. Bruce was paying the price for his delinquency.

'How is he?' Gemma enquired, politeness rather than any real concern prompting her enquiry. She didn't honestly care what Bruce felt. She felt drained of all emotion, after her ordeal.

Stefan lifted an eyebrow, 'He'll recover,' he said not unkindly. He signalled to the bartender for another whisky as if any further mention of Bruce was distasteful to him.

'Should you?' Gemma asked tactlessly. She had not meant it to sound like that. All she wanted to do was to rest her head on his chest and tell him how she was indebted to him. But

122

it did not come out like that.

Stefan looked at her for one long, hard moment, then deliberately swallowed several fingers of the liquid before saying, 'I wonder if you know how inappropriate that sort of remark is,' he said quietly. 'Baxter may not know how to hold his drink but then men like him hardly ever do. All hot air, no substance and clearly no gentleman. But obviously the sort of man universally loved by women. Don't ask me why—it's quite incomprehensible to me.'

His remark irritated her, but she was too exhausted to counter it or get into an argument with him. She stifled a yawn and stumbled to her feet. 'Thank you again,' she said awkwardly. It was quite inadequate, she knew that, but what else could she say to someone who had sprung her from the jaws of death?

Stefan's clear green eyes rested on her in a way that made the blood rush to her cheeks. She looked away uncertainly, her heart pounding.

'Be careful,' he chided her softly, a gleam to his eyes. 'Next time, you might not survive to tell the tale.'

'There won't be a next time,' Gemma assured him sleepily.

He looked sceptical, a crooked smile on his face. 'That's what they all say. Well, goodnight then.' He walked to the door and paused. 'By the way, your helmet—your . . . talisman. Your saviour. If I hadn't popped back with it, you'd have spent the night out in the North Sea. I've left it at reception.' He pushed open the front door and presently she heard the Volvo disappear into the night.

Gemma undressed as if in a trance, numbed by the events of the day; it was a calm, if somewhat damp summer evening. She threw open the window and leaned out breathing in deeply the smell of the rain-soaked earth. To think that she might never have been able to do that again! Her brush with the grim reaper made her flesh creep and she shut the window, retreating to the swaddling comfort of the bed. It was a grisly thought. She curled up in a ball of self-defence, her sleep fitful, interrupted, the nightmare so real that several times she woke in a cold sweat.

CHAPTER FIVE

Stefan's Summer party was bound to be a glittering occasion, Gemma reckoned. Earlier that day she had popped into her uncle's house for a whirlwind check. Mrs Moore urged on her freshly brewed Blue Mountain coffee and her home-made cherry cake. 'Mr Wells never liked to miss Mr Stefan's parties,' she revealed to an astonished Gemma who never imagined her uncle would have turned out on a summer evening for any social event unless it was connected with business or 'charity', in which case he would regard it as 'work'—a duty to be done and to be seen to be done willingly.

' "What a wonderful host Stefan is!" he used to say and it would put him in a good mood for the rest of the week. Every year, after the party, he would say to me afterwards, "I shall give one of my own," but when he settled down to work out the details, he just used to abandon the whole idea. Not for him, professional party planners swooping down to transform his home as they did for Mr Stefan and altering it to something unrecognisable. So, he never got around to it.'

That evening, Gemma knew she had never looked lovelier; her red hair coiled up in an elegant loop contrasted strikingly with the sheer black of the mid-calf length dress with its hand beaded lace bodice, low-scooped neckline and swirling taffeta skirt. The heavy antique silver choker with its mysterious design of stars and flowers winked in the night—it had been a present from Uncle— brought back from Central Africa after a rare exotic holiday one year. The hotel had ordered a taxi to take her to the party but tonight, of all nights, it was late in arriving.

The party was in full swing when the cab drew up. The transformation of Stefan's very English walled garden to Moorish garden was so utterly complete that it seemed as if she had stepped back in time. There were strategically placed cypresses and the fragrance of damask rose petals filled the air, the dry stone walls cleverly disguised to resemble faintly roseate whitewashed walls, covered with a confection of tiles and stucco and a subtly lighted arcaded patio enclosed a gently gushing fountain.

'My dear, you look divine.' She was surprised to see Mr Hanson—but then why shouldn't he have been invited? He was a vital link between Stefan and Uncle Arthur. Mr Hanson came forward, greeting her with a kiss on the cheek. He drew her to one side, skilfully plucking two glasses of champagne from the tray of a passing white-aproned waitress. His bald head gleamed, making him look like a Roman senator.

'How very nice to see you,' Gemma smiled back at him. They exchanged pleasantries and Gemma told him about Speedwell.

'Stefan did say you'd grasped the nettle!' He gave her some helpful tips. 'Well my dear— much as I have enjoyed talking to you, we shall have to do our duty, as Arthur would have said, and circulate.' He detached himself from her.

Gemma moved to the edge of the garden. She had seen Pavel and Marianne unobtrusively keeping an eye on the hired staff but there was no one else apart from Mr Hanson that she recognised. A contingent of

126

Romanians, a number of well-to-do local landowners—she heard someone introduced as an earl—and the rest seemed to represent every nationality in Europe. It was a wonderful and stimulating polyglot mix. She smiled to herself.

'Share the joke?' Stefan had come up behind her so quietly he made her jump. He looked amazingly attractive in evening dress, the formality of his attire somehow enhancing his magnetism.

'You startled me!' she exclaimed.

'You startle easily,' he returned. 'Don't you expect the host to be present?' He put his hand under her elbow and guided her over to the fountain. 'Or perhaps you think the party would go with more of a swing if the party-giver stayed away?' His gaze swept appreciatively over her, lingering on the deep cleft of her bosom. 'I'm certainly no ghost.' She could feel his charm beginning to work and looked away, ignoring the humorous green eyes.

'My guests probably would, but you're the reason why they've all come,' she said, her tone sincere.

She glanced at him as, with a dry martini in one hand, his eyes roamed over the animated gathering—judging, appraising, although his expression was smoothly blank.

For a moment he seemed uncharacter-istically at a loss for words. 'Come on,' he said at last, his hand resting momentarily on her fragrant newly washed hair. 'Meet some of the others. Let's start with the Carltons.'

'What a good idea,' Gemma agreed lightly. Their conversation wasn't exactly sparkling, she thought drily.

'Hello, Lyse.' He stopped and addressed a young woman, 'I haven't seen you since half-term,' he remarked. Under the girl's surface glitz, Gemma suspected she was no more than seventeen. Lyse glowered at her with undisguised distaste, a poisonous-looking concoction in her cocktail glass. She did not like to be reminded that she was still a schoolgirl, often going to the other extreme. Quite unlike me, Gemma thought, remembering herself at the same age—her unbecoming scrawniness and her total lack of guile. Lyse looked at least twenty-five tonight; her thick black hair with its polished low lights swung round her jawline, the scarlet designer catsuit with the deep plunge back and front fitted snugly to her precociously voluptuous body. Gemma sensed the girl's sudden irrational dislike of her. Lyse probably saw her as a rival for Stefan's affections for she could see no other reason for her to have earned the girl's adolescent contempt. Lyse gazed mesmerised at Stefan, her arm now possessively hooked through his, her long, artificial eyelashes fluttering. She turned her back on Gemma, deliberately snubbing her.

Above Lyse's head, Stefan's mouth curved in amusement as he listened to her inane chatter with what seemed total absorption, skilfully persuading the girl to swap her alcoholic drink for a cocktail of fresh fruit juice.

'Stefan and I are old friends,' Lyse remarked loftily. She gave him a quick flirtatious look, her moist lips parted.

'So it seems,' Gemma's voice was laced with sarcasm and she stared at Stefan who looked on indulgently.

'What do you mean by that?' Lyse demanded. Her lower lip quivered and she detached herself from Stefan and moved towards Gemma, her hard hazel eyes narrowing with anger. 'You'll regret that.'

Gemma stared bewildered. Lyse raised her hand slightly and for one awful moment Gemma thought she was going to strike her. Stefan quickly intervened, linking the girl's fingers in his, smoothly averting what could have been a nasty incident.

'Let's go and find your dad,' he suggested to her, his green eyes coaxing. Lyse hesitated, her thought processes quite transparent, Gemma observed. She did not want to be returned to the bosom of her family. She wanted to be monopolised all evening by Stefan. But if she did not accompany him now, he would drift off and leave her with Gemma and that she certainly did not want. Lyse unleashed the full glory of her smile on him and, clinging to him like a second skin, she allowed him to waft her off. Gemma looked after them, mute irritation mingled with a desire to laugh out loud. There was something so melodramatic about Lyse it was almost comic. Stefan suddenly glanced back over his shoulder, his mouth wry, laughter lurking in his eyes, his shoulders shaking in a quiet chuckle. He turned back his head, bending to meet Lyse's in a secret conspiratorial way.

Gemma retreated to the cloakroom to powder her nose and renewed her rose-pink lipstick before she returned to the party which showed no signs of slowing up. With relief she noticed that an older woman, probably Lyse's mother, had prised her daughter away from Stefan and, from the mutinous expression on the girl's face, it seemed she was being quietly rebuked. Later, out of the corner of her eye as she disengaged herself from the straying hands of a Spanish fabric designer, she saw Lyse hustled away by her parents. The band struck up a tango and the Spaniard re-advanced on her but before he could swing her round to the beat, Stefan stepped out of the shadows.

'Host's privilege,' he said breezily and the Spaniard shrugged his shoulders good-humouredly and went in search of his wife.

Gemma was very conscious of Stefan's hard, muscular body against hers, trying to tell herself that it was not that but the cumulative effect of the evening's alcohol which was passing a message to her stomach and her loins. She flushed and said, her voice rising a little, 'Try your cave man tactics on someone else.'

He gathered her closer to him and whispered in her ear, 'I want you to do something for me. You owe me a favour, remember?'

Gemma's head was in a whirl, 'I don't get your drift. What can I do for you?'

He released her only when the music ended, his face dark, his mouth set hard.

'You're coming with me to my study.' His eyes were suddenly very pale, and they glittered dangerously. The veneer of the cultivated sociable man swept aside. He thrust his hand through his hair, the other reached out to grip her elbow, his fingers closing on her arm like a vice. He hurried her into the house—the sound of the band and the party guests grew fainter as he rushed her through one lighted room after another until they came to his book-lined study. He locked the door and she could feel the tension in him, his breath coming in uneven jerks.

'You're drunk!' Gemma almost said, seeing the passion buried in the winter of his eyes, the angle of the light on his face accentuating the planed-down flesh of the cheekbones. Now that he knew that he had engaged her attention, the tension inside him began to ebb away.

'Lyse,' he said simply.

Gemma opened and shut her mouth. 'Lyse?' she repeated incredulously. She couldn't see the relevance.

'Yes. Lyse, Lyse, Lyse Carlton.' He accompanied it by four thumps of his fist on the desk. 'She is a teenage werewolf and if her parents—old friends of mine—and I don't do something quickly, I shall find myself defending them on a murder charge when Lyse's body is found in one of the ponds on my estate. She is going through that stage of adolescence which is driving her parents into a nervous breakdown.'

'But what do you want me to do? How can I help? She detests me, that's obvious.'

Stefan was very close to her, his breath fluttering the tendrils of her hair. He drew her towards him, an arm encircling her waist, his warm smell mingling with the scent of the French perfume she wore. A fierce surge of anger flowed through her and she put up her fists to fend him off. She did not want him to make love to her like this. He caught her wrists in his free hand, and lowered his head to kiss the cleft between her breasts. Despite herself, she could feel her nipples hardening. He was drunk. She was sure of that.

'Don't—please stop.' But her plea was cut short by his mouth against hers. All her resistance was nothing to the heat of his lips on hers and the urgent exploration of his tongue. He lifted his head, the emerald of his eyes glittering like those of a cat's in the dark.

'I'll tell you what I want,' he said lazily, tilting her chin. 'What I've wanted from the moment I first saw you—'

'You're crazy!' Gemma's voice sounded to her like a hoarse whisper. 'You're pissed. You don't know what you want. But I do. I want out of here.' The shadows in the room were flying and dancing but his grip on her merely tightened as she tried to detach herself, the brush of his stomach against her awakening the primitive currents of her emotions. At last he set her free and crossed to a chair by the window. He met her confused and angry gaze with a faint, lopsided smile.

'I want to send Lyse to you for a couple of weeks,' he announced calmly.

Gemma turned away, sick with fury. 'We're fully booked—anyway from her performance tonight she's likely to be totally disruptive. I couldn't have that. You can't compel her to go if she doesn't want to. Besides,' Gemma gave a slightly triumphant smile, 'even if I could find room for her I doubt if she'd come.' Stefan couldn't force Lyse on her if the accommodation didn't stretch to it.

'I've considered all that. The hotel does keep one or two spare rooms for casual guests. I checked. She can occupy one of those. Her parents will gladly pay the supplement.'

He had it all carefully thought out, Gemma thought grimly. He was determined to foist the girl on her. Well, with a bit of luck, Lyse would abscond after a few days. But how was he going to persuade her to join Speedwell in the first place, she wondered?

Stefan answered the unspoken question. 'She'll come.' He added confidently. 'It's all done by bribery and corruption,' he gave her a quick smile. Gemma addressed the rug under her black velvet pumps. It seemed she had no choice in the matter.

'When can I expect her?' she said resignedly.

'Her parents will run her over tomorrow before they return to London.'

Gemma rounded on him, 'You're a swine! So that's why you invited me to your party.' She stood up and smoothed down her dress. Her legs shivered uncontrollably as if they were about to give way.

'No, Gemma. The invitation had no ulterior motive,' Stefan said in a steady tone. 'You've got to believe that.' He gently touched her arm.

Gemma felt too jaded to argue with him.

'All right then but if she gives any trouble, she'll be out on her ear,' she warned him.

He threw back his head and laughed. 'She's been expelled from too many schools to let that worry her!'

The glamorous sex kitten of the night before had reverted to scruffy teenager. Gemma imagined there had been the usual adolescent skirmishing with her parents that morning for Lyse turned up at the driving wheel of Stefan's XJ6, L-plates dangling from the back, with Stefan in the front passenger seat. She fixed him with a lingering dewy look, and flung her arms round him, burying her fingers in his hair.

'Come on—let's make a move.' Stefan removed himself from her embrace, sliding away from her. He dumped her holdall on the floor of the entrance hall.

'Have a good time, Lyse.' The girl's eyes filled with easy tears. Gemma looked on with mounting irritation and cursed Stefan for fuelling the girl's teenage fantasies. She gritted her teeth. He was stroking her hair and murmuring God knows what to the girl whose breast was rising and falling theatrically.

'I'll show you to your room,' Gemma gently touched Lyse's arm. Lyse shivered melodramatically.

'Bye beautiful,' Stefan kissed the girl on the brow. A devilish look came into his eyes.

'Do you really think so?' Lyse, insecure, adolescent, was overcome by the compliment. She put her arms round his neck. Stefan adroitly peeled her off. 'Plenty of time for this

135

later. Now I want you to promise me something—'

For a few wild seconds Gemma felt sorry for Lyse.

'I'll do anything for you—promise,' Lyse said unsuspectingly.

'I want you to enjoy yourself. Remember you're doing it for me.'

Lyse's face was a picture of dashed anticipation and mute acceptance of the inevitable. She began to whine but he pressed his finger to her lips and cut her short. Then without a backward glance he walked swiftly to the car and spun it away. The girl's eyes were glued to its retreating body, her face mirroring a mixture of emotions.

*   *   *

Stefan had left nothing to chance, Gemma thought grumpily. Lyse was equipped with a motor-cyclist's learner driver licence and an expensive, designer crash helmet. The first few days were difficult. Lyse morosely refused to join the others and mooched about the grounds or spent time making long and expensive telephone calls to her friends far and wide. Then an overheard remark by one of the bikers about her favourite pop singer challenging his assumption to be the greatest saw her participating and she seemed to take to some of the bikers rough and ready ways.

136

As pillion passenger or intrepid biker she went on the daily outings and trips to the local disco with gusto.

'There's a message for Lyse to call her dad,' the receptionist announced one morning.

'I'll take it up to her before she goes out,' Gemma promised. She had woken with a streaming cold and a blinding headache and decided against accompanying the bikers to a picnic. Gemma was sure it was flu. She rose to her feet from the armchair and knocked on Lyse's bedroom door.

'Yeah,' came the grudging response.

Gemma entered the room, and blanched at its untidiness. Clothes, albums, cassettes, empty coca cola cans lay strewn around. On the dressing-table lay a pile of new, obviously unread paperbacks—probably a holiday reading list provided by a well-meaning English teacher. Chekhov, Oscar Wilde, Dostoevsky, Philip Larkin, Laurens van der Post—all clearly left Lyse quite cold.

It dawned on Gemma that Lyse had no academic bent but her well-meaning parents refused to acknowledge that to themselves and were determined to push her into A-levels and university. No wonder there was so much family conflict.

Lyse grunted when Gemma handed her the telephone message. Gemma made a private bet with herself that she would not return the call.

'I'm staying in the hotel today,' Gemma told her. Lyse did not react but continued to assemble her gear.

Gemma repeated herself.

Lyse stared at her and then shrugged her shoulders, 'Suit yourself.' She made for the stairs and Gemma closed the door on the battle-scarred room.

Gemma waved the bikers off and collapsed weakly in the armchair. She had never felt so rotten in her life. Her legs felt like water and the staircase had never seemed so long when eventually she struggled up to her room. She drew the bedclothes round her and fell into a feverish sleep. Several loud knocks on the door roused her. It was the receptionist. She peered anxiously into the room.

'They are half way through supper. There was no sign of you. That's strange, I thought, so here I am.' Unbidden, she entered the room. 'Heavens, you look absolutely done. Shouldn't I call the doctor?'

Gemma nodded. Her body ached all over. Although she tried to avoid falling into the clutches of the medical profession, she knew now that she had no choice.

The receptionist left, promising to have a light meal sent up.

'Bed rest for you for the next few days and I forbid you to go out for at least a week,' the local doctor said as he wrote out a prescription for antibiotics.

Gemma struggled to sit up, 'I can't take off so much time,' she protested weakly, pushing back the hair from her eyes.

He sat on the side of the bed. 'You must do as you're told,' he said bluntly. 'Either you hit it now, good and strong, or it will fell you. It'll lead to complications and you'll find yourself spending even longer recuperating.'

'But I have to be out and about—Speedwell demands it.' Gemma had to make him understand.

'Speedwell demands that you recover,' he reiterated firmly. 'Now, I'll call again in a few days' time. In the meantime, make sure you take the pills regularly and remember to finish the course.' He looked at her gravely, 'Miss Wells—I am not exaggerating. You are suffering from a very virulent and particularly nasty strain of influenza. If you don't tackle it as I suggest, the consequences will be very serious for you.'

Gemma fell back on the pillow, defeated, tears pricking the back of her eyelids. It couldn't have come at a worse moment. This was the height of Speedwell's season. She had to be up and about supervising and participating. It was no use asking Pip to come up and help. She knew her friend couldn't. As a free-lance cook, the summer months were her busiest time.

Gemma heard a noise and looked up. Lyse lolled against the doorpost chewing gum.

139

'Great day,' she moved the gum to the inside of her left cheek. Her eyes roamed curiously over Gemma. 'You ill?'

Gemma felt like laughing out loud and realised she was on the verge of hysteria. She took a deep breath and put Lyse quickly in the picture.

'No sweat,' Lyse said. 'Leave it to me,' and in that moment Gemma could have sworn that the girl relished being in charge. She was too weak to argue with her. She felt so tired that her muscles refused to relax.

'I need to know what's going on—if there are any problems . . .'

Lyse nodded vigorously, 'Yea, yea, but there won't be.'

Gemma gazed at her anxiously, telling herself she was mad to rely on Lyse. But she had no alternative.

Gemma lost count of time over the next few days, neither caring nor wanting to know the date or the day of the week. On the eighth day after she had been ordered to bed by the doctor, she woke feeling completely new. Cautiously she swung her legs to the floor and gazed at her reflection in the mirror. Although her face was pale and there were dark circles under her eyes, she had lost that haggard look. She dressed quickly and went into the breakfast room. It buzzed with conversation and laughter. Now that she could actually savour the tang in the marmalade, Gemma ate several pieces of thickly buttered hot toast. It seemed that her absence had scarcely been noticed or missed. Lyse strolled over to her and pulled out a chair.

'Everything's under control.'

And it certainly seemed like that to Gemma. There were no bikers queueing with a catalogue of complaints or crowding round her to enquire what was planned for the day. Lyse rose to her feet. 'Got to go—see you later.' It was the signal for the others to follow and they trooped after her, joking and jostling each other.

Gemma waited till they had all left and made her way to the reception desk.

'You look much better,' the receptionist told her.

'I feel it,' Gemma remarked, adding almost as an afterthought, 'any problems I ought to know about?'

The receptionist shook her head. 'Lyse took to it like a duck to water. Seemed to enjoy bossing them about and they didn't mind. Popular girl, too. She had them eating out of her hand in no time. And a dab hand as a mechanic. No hesitation in rolling up her sleeves and getting some of those old jalopies on the road again when they broke down. And what energy. And if all that riding about during the day was not enough, she had them riding about at night—moonlight picnics, no less.'

It seemed to Gemma that at last Lyse had found what she wanted to do and it was nothing to do with academia.

It was a transformed Lyse who entered the lounge with her holdall when Stefan was announced.

'Hi,' she said casually. Gemma was surprised at the low-key greeting. She did not present her lips for a kiss or bury her head on Stefan's chest.

'It was great.' Her eyes shone. 'The best part was telling them what to do and seeing them do it. Then I had this groovy plan to pool all our ideas. That really gave us lift-off. They said I was brilliant. And it was real fun mending some of those bikes. I liked working with my hands. Fantastic!'

'So you were the toast of Speedwell!' Stefan teased her gently.

Lyse blushed with becoming modesty and turned to Gemma, 'I'm coming back next year—I wouldn't miss it for the world. Then I'm going to start up my own bike repair shop.'

Stefan fastened his seat belt. 'You've worked a miracle,' he said so softly so that only Gemma could hear, 'but then I always knew you would,' he added with a mischievous grin. He slipped the clutch and gave an easy wave of his hand.

CHAPTER SIX

'Business is still brisk, I'm glad to report,' Pip gave her a Cheshire-cat grin. For Gemma's sake she was glad that her friend's enterprise showed no cracks or other signs of premature decline.

'You've definitely carved a niche for yourself in the holiday market. Look,' she held up a daily newspaper and pointed to its travel page. 'You've been given full marks here'. She read aloud the two-column report of the action packed holiday with Speedwell which its intrepid reporter had spent incognito. 'His name doesn't tally with those on the reservations list. He must have registered under an alias.'

Gemma reached out for the paper and scanned the feature for herself, feeling immensely proud of the commendation. It was September; only five months into her business venture and she was more than holding her own.

'Has Stefan been fed any monthly figures yet?' she enquired anxiously, drumming her fingers on the table. She hadn't forgotten that she was accountable to him. He was supposed to be monitoring Speedwell's progress.

Pip's response was prompt, and Gemma warmed to her conscientiousness. 'Not to worry. He's had a bundle of papers every month and I even submitted a quarterly profit and loss account. But absolutely no feedback from him. Just a brief acknowledgement from the clerk in chambers. Without his input though, it's difficult to assess if he thinks you're doing well or badly. One doesn't know what yardstick he'll use. But anyway he can't accuse you of dereliction of duty.'

'That's the problem,' Gemma agreed mournfully. 'I'm sort of groping in the dark. I think the figures are healthy. I'm certainly not running at a loss and unless there's a totally unexpected downturn, I know we're going to end up with a substantial turnover. But is it going to be good enough for Stefan?'

Pip frowned. 'But surely,' she queried acidly, 'so long as you don't end up owing anything to anybody, that's all that matters? What else could he possibly expect during the first year's trading? Anything over and above that is a wonderful bonus. He can't expect a multi-million turnover,' she added sarcastically. 'Anyway from what you told me, your uncle didn't expect you to make a killing before you could inherit, only that you make a go of the business. And you've done that.'

Gemma sighed, and ran her fingers distractedly through her hair. 'That's what worries me. I'm sure uncle didn't intend it as a matter of win or lose, but how I played the game. But the gloss Stefan puts on it might

144

well be different, and if I don't measure up to his expectation, whatever that may be, I might never come into Uncle's bequest. It seems a no-win situation.'

Pip stared at her and pushed back a lock of her thick, brown hair. 'No, that wouldn't be fair.' She shook her head vehemently. 'He can't make the rules as he goes along.'

'Can't he?' Gemma gave her friend a wintry smile. 'I can't stop him. If I don't measure up to his idea of success, then so be it. I'm not doing so badly anyway. I'll make it on my own without that millstone of an inheritance round my neck.' She hurriedly flicked through the paper as if searching for something. 'That's what I'm looking for. I thought I saw it featured this time last week.'

Pip craned over her shoulder, 'An application form for the Young Entrepreneur of the Year Award. Are you going to enter?'

'You bet!' Gemma grinned as she uttered the widely used Americanism. 'I'll just be able to make the closing date if I fill it in now. Then we'll go and treat ourselves at Peggy's.'

Gemma popped the sealed envelope through the pillarbox on their way to Peggy's which was a well-known bakery in the town— old-fashioned and comforting behind its Georgian shopfront, its cakes and pastries were legendary and people flocked from far and wide to meet and munch at its little circular tables. Although there was a longish queue, it was fast moving and they were soon seated. They ordered a pot of tea and a mouth-watering selection of sumptuous home-made cakes. It was market day and the tea-room was crowded with farmers and dealers. Gemma glanced round and waved, as she recognised a few familiar faces.

'Who's Stefan with?' Pip asked, her mouth full.

Gemma looked across to the slim, fair-haired young woman who was pouring out tea for him. Her heart thudded uneasily. She shook her head and busied herself with a piece of chocolate gâteau. 'Never seen her before.' It gave her a nasty turn to see Stefan with some other woman. A curious unsettled feeling invaded her. 'Looks his type though,' she dug her fork into the gâteau with unnecessary force. Suddenly she could not bear to be in the same room as them. It was unbearable, hearing, if not seeing them laugh and joke together in animated companionship.

Pip resumed her interested appraisal of the couple then scanned her friend's face thoughtfully. Was it her imagination or did she detect a certain bleakness in Gemma's expression? It was quickly replaced by a clever imitation of indifference. Too indifferent, Pip decided. She doesn't fool me. It was crystal clear to her at that moment that Gemma had fallen in love with her trustee. A love so it seemed that was not reciprocated. Stefan had

146

not seen them.

Too engrossed in his lady love, Pip thought exasperated, feeling sorry for Gemma. What a mess!

Gemma was disinclined to linger now that she had seen Stefan and his woman companion. What should have been a pleasant outing, a break from 'minding the shop' had turned to ashes in her mouth. She hurriedly swallowed her cup of tea, the hot liquid scalding the back of her throat. She left the half-eaten gâteau on the plate and dabbed her mouth with a paper napkin. Muttering to Pip that she had a headache, she pushed back her chair. Pip rose to her feet. She didn't need to be told how Gemma felt. Despite her best efforts to put on a brave face and to disguise the intensity of her feelings for Stefan, she knew Gemma had taken it hard. Pip cast one longing look at the remaining cream horn and cursed Stefan again. On the rare occasion Gemma allowed herself time off in what had been some fiendishly busy weeks, it was ruined by extraneous events. It was too late for second thoughts. Their table was being cleared ready for a patiently waiting mother and her toddler. She hurried through the door after her.

Gemma mounted her bike without a word or a backward glance and roared off, oblivious to whether or not Pip kept up with her. She let it rip, and Pip, finding it difficult to keep apace, soon fell behind. The speed was cathartic and by the time Gemma had arrived back at the hotel, she felt that some of the tension had melted away. But she had to admit to herself what she had long suppressed or denied. She was in love with Stefan.

'I suppose that's the best thing,' she grinned ruefully at herself in the hall mirror. 'Now I know the problem, how do I deal with it? 'In a bygone age, the cure would have been a long cruise to far-flung countries. Her bruised heart would have mended and she would have forged other friendships. But that was impossible. Her life was inextricably bound up with Stefan's for the foreseeable future, at any rate.

*   *   *

'This arrived for you by recorded delivery, this morning.' The receptionist handed her an official-looking buff envelope and Gemma signed for it. The woman craned her neck to read the contents as she slid the flap open with a thumb nail. Gemma smiled to herself and slipped the single folded sheet of writing-paper into her trouser pocket. Nosy woman! She ran up the long flight of stairs to her room. Anticipation made her heart beat faster than usual. She sat on the bed, withdrew the letter from her pocket and began to read it. At first the contents did not register. She read it again slowly, scarcely able to take it in. 'You are one of six contenders shortlisted for the Young Entrepreneur of the Year Award.' The letter went on to invite her to compete in the final round which was to be held in London in a fortnight's time. The contenders would be interviewed by a panel of judges, their efforts assessed, each contender would then have to give a brief presentation describing their business and their achievements to a studio audience and then the panel would make the award. The presentation and the award giving would be televised for maximum exposure.

Gemma heard Pip's bike cruising down the drive and could hardly wait to tell her. Even to be shortlisted was tremendously exciting. There had initially been a great number of candidates and competition had been very stiff. The letter assured those unselected that failure to be shortlisted did not reflect either on their business or their ability. She forced herself to a sedate pace down the stairs and steered her friend into the lounge, which was mercifully deserted.

Pip waltzed Gemma round the room when she broke the news. 'You've done it!' she exulted.

'There's still a long way to go,' Gemma cautioned. 'I may have got through the heats but the finals are what matters.' But secretly she felt over the moon. In her present shifting moods, it was the best surprise she could have hoped for. She read the letter again. The other five finalists—one woman and three men, were older than she was in age and experience. She tried to recollect what they looked like, but her memory failed her, save for the woman. There hadn't been many women entrants. Gemma recalled that the other woman finalist was assured, smart-looking and very confident.

'But what about Speedwell? I can't just leave it and expect it to run itself.' In all the euphoria, she had almost forgotten that she had a business to mind. She turned anxiously to Pip.

Her friend had pre-empted her and was already consulting her electronic diary.

'You're born under a lucky star,' she told Gemma. 'The competition is scheduled to take place on those few days between bookings. Remember?' She keyed in a few formulae and nodded. 'Yes. I've made absolutely sure, there's nothing to stop you from going.'

Gemma breathed a sigh of relief. 'The conflict would have been too terrible. I'd never have been able to resolve it satisfactorily. Now I don't need to.'

Pip said warningly, 'You're far too conscientious. I'd have made time for the competition. Lucky you weren't torn between the two. I can guess where your priorities would lie.'

* * *

Gemma returned to her Blackheath flat a day before she was due at the hotel where all the finalists were being accommodated. It was wonderful to be home again she thought with affection as she placed a vase of chrysanthemums on the dining-room table. Blackheath was beautiful at this time of the year, but then it had a perennial charm. In Winter, it was a like a scene from an old Dutch painting—the heath glistening with hoar frost and the ponds frozen over. In Summer, the sky above was a patchwork of multi-coloured kites flown by children; in Spring it was like a showground with the annual Easter fair. Now it was October, when chestnut sellers stood by the gates of Greenwich Park, and the smell of conkers roasting on an open fire mingled with the scent of fallen Autumn leaves.

The hotel was large and modern near the television studios in Shepherds Bush. Gemma thought it looked like an army barracks. She was escorted to her bedroom by a smartly dressed bellboy solemnly carrying her small case. It was a large room, comfortably furnished in 'contract furniture' style. She visualised hundreds of like rooms furnished in the same vein—a characterless anonymity with no thought of adding that extra ingredient— that 'something'—that would lend a unique personal touch. It had an *en suite* bathroom, tiled from top to bottom in shiny mirror tiles.

Gemma ran the bath and while it filled, she gazed critically at herself, naked. She seemed to have lost a lot of weight over the past few weeks; her cheeks had become quite hollow although she felt healthy enough.

Next morning she met the other contenders. 'The condemned man eats a hearty breakfast,' mused Gemma ruefully as she observed the others desultorily nibbling at toast and leaving half finished cups of coffee. Gemma tucked into bacon and eggs with an appetite which surprised even herself.

They were taken in a mini-van to the television centre, studiously avoiding conversation with each other. Skilled make-up ladies worked quickly and expertly to prepare them for the glare of the television arc lights. As they stepped onto the stage, Gemma sensed the highly charged atmosphere. Her pulses started to race.

The adjudication panel consisted of three middle-aged men, and a well preserved woman of indeterminate age, all captains of industry in their own special fields. The presenter was a household name—Kevin Ampthill. He was debonair, handsome and a bachelor. The winner, if a woman, would be invited to dine with him, whereas if the winner was male, his counterpart, an equally illustrious woman television personality would do the honours. To save precious viewing time, the oral examination of all the finalists by the panel had taken place privately the day before. Kevin Ampthill effortlessly introduced contestants to the viewing public and the studio audience, giving a pithy biographical sketch of each as the cameras switched from face to face.

Gemma wore an ankle-length, long-sleeved emerald green velvet dress with a ruffled lace neckline, her red hair swept up and caught in the centre of her head with a mother-of-pearl comb. Excitement and nervous tension brought the right touch of colour to her cheeks. Kevin Ampthill's job now was to show them to the viewing public and the studio audience in the shortest space of time without seeming to hustle them. He was excellent at his job, Gemma observed admiringly. Everything slid along like a well-oiled machine and, if there were any hitches he skated smoothly over them. She sat enthralled as he adroitly conversed with each candidate, putting them at ease and laughing and joking with them as he lobbed his probing questions as if he had all the time in the world. No wonder he was so successful and commanded such high fees. He had totally mastered the medium.

Gemma enjoyed talking to him; she began to unwind and soon they were exchanging banter as if they were firm friends enjoying each other's company over a drink in the sitting-room of her flat. Gemma responded to his adept handling of her, now quite unconscious of the lynx-eyed assessors. Then the moment which was every candidate's private nightmare arrived. A brief personal presentation of his business to the viewers. The two men who preceded her sounded confident and accomplished and earned themselves prolonged applause. It would be a hard act to follow, she thought morosely, her tensions returning. When her name was called, she moved centre stage like a puppet to the spot which Kevin Ampthill directed her to. The presentation had had to be memorised as no scripts were permitted.

Gemma started quietly, hesitantly, a great contrast after the two men who had both turned out assured, well-crafted appearances. She described her business as simply as she could, gingering it up by confessing to the mishaps which had befallen her. To her surprise, there were gales of laughter, but in the main, she thought her speech, so ordinary, and so lack-lustre compared with her rivals that she wondered how she could possibly have been shortlisted. The laughter was encouraging and, although the studio audience seemed to warm to her anecdotes, the applause was polite but not over-enthusiastic. She looked out into the audience for moral support. Pip was there, somewhere, she knew that, with a few other friends. Bruce had heard about the competition and had insisted that he

154

would be there as a seasoned entrepreneur with 1001 words of advice. Thankfully, Gemma had managed to miss him and the audience was just a sea of faces. The panel huddled together whispering and consulting their notes. The wait was agonising. Gemma felt sick with apprehension and tried to remind herself that it was not a matter of life and death, but to no avail. Then Kevin Ampthill stepped forward into the spotlight once more, the same lazy smile on his lips.

'Ladies and Gentlemen. Now is the moment we've all been waiting for. Without further ado, let me announce the winners, in reverse order, of the competition to find the Young Entrepreneur of the Year.' There was an explosion of applause as the names of the third prize winner and the runner-up were announced. Both looked disappointed at first at not having achieved the ultimate but this was soon replaced with pleasure as they mounted the rostrum and were each presented with cash awards and a small commemorative medal. Both men, they beamed and bowed before returning to their seats. The atmosphere in the studio was electric with expectation. Gemma folded her hands in her lap, feeling anything but composed; she could feel her heart beating in her stomach.

Kevin Ampthill said briefly, almost matter of factly, 'The Young Entrepreneur of the Year is Gemma Wells of Speedwell Holidays.'

The announcement was followed by a spontaneous outburst of clapping and cheering. He beckoned to Gemma. She could not believe it and for a moment sat rivetted to her chair. Then as the camera swung towards her she stood up and walked to take her place beside him. The chairman of the panel made a congratulatory speech and presented her with a cheque for £1000 and a silver bowl engraved with figures of toiling humans. Stunned, Gemma managed a few modest words of thanks. She had not expected to win so she had not thought to prepare anything remotely resembling an acceptance speech. She took a deep breath and turned hesitantly to Kevin Ampthill for inspiration. He gave her a wide encouraging smile, his curly golden hair shining under the bright lights.

She said simply, 'This is really quite incredible. It's like a dream from which I'm sure I'm going to awake and find that Speedwell Holidays has gone down the tube.'

And then the closing chords of the signature tune which had opened the show sounded and it was all over. Kevin Ampthill ushered them all backstage where there were renewed congratulations. Members of the audience, friends and relatives crowded round to add their good wishes.

Pip bounced up to greet her, followed closely by several other friends.

'Well done, I knew you'd pull it off,' Pip

156

bellowed at her above the pell-mell.

'That's more than I did,' Gemma shouted back. It was wonderful to have a friend like Pip who never for one moment doubted Gemma's ability to take Speedwell to new heights.

Gemma saw Bruce elbowing his way through the cluster of well-wishers, his face bright red with triumph.

'Oh no,' Gemma groaned inwardly, 'not him.' She averted her face, deliberately engaging a complete stranger in animated conversation and suddenly became aware of a tall figure at her shoulder.

'So Germander Speedwell flourishes anew in alien soil,' Stefan said very softly in her ear.

Gemma looked up at him, her heart hammering in her chest like a caged bird. 'You!' she exclaimed involuntarily. He was the last person she expected to be present, dismissing as he no doubt would her 'flirtations' with such frivolity. Too superficial, he would probably say, not the sort of thing a budding businessman should be wasting his time on.

'Who else?' he rejoined, 'or should I say, at your service Madam Managing Director? Congratulations. It was well deserved.'

The praise and the tone in which it was spoken were warm and genuinely heartfelt. Gemma blushed as his eyes caught hers and held them for several long moments.

Stefan continued, speaking so low that she

157

had to move closer to him to catch his words. 'It's a fitting end to your enterprise, don't you think?'

The end! The sound of it made her gasp for breath. It was like being hit in the solar plexus and for a moment she gazed wildly at him. Put so bluntly and without any sort of prologue it sounded so utterly final. Yes, it was the end. Not just the end of six months' hard slog, albeit crowned with success, but the end, inevitably enough, of her involvement with Stefan. She steadied her voice, brushing a stray strand of hair from her eyes. 'The end, yes . . . but also the beginning of . . .' Before she could finish, her hand was seized.

'Wonderful, Gem. I knew you'd scoop the pools. Great news, isn't it Radulescu?' It was a rhetorical question Pip thought, as she raised her eyebrows resignedly at Gemma. Bruce did not care one bit whether Stefan agreed with him or not.

Bruce rattled on, full of his own importance, convincing himself that he had masterminded the whole thing. 'Do you know, some of the credit must go to me. I told her just what to say and how to say it.' It was so patently untrue that Pip and Stefan burst out laughing. Bruce looked puzzled. Gemma was too flushed with her own victory to care very much. Bruce leaned forward to kiss her on the lips and Gemma moved her head slightly so that his mouth caught the edge of her cheek.

Stefan said quietly, 'I couldn't see any signs of your coaching in Gemma's presentation and perhaps it was just as well, it had the touch of the true amateur about it. Natural and unpretentious.'

But it made no difference to Bruce. 'That's what I am trying to say,' he said a trifle impatiently. He still held Gemma's hand. 'All those weeks I spent in that god-forsaken hotel in the north paid off for her. I gave her a good many tips then and see, it certainly paid off. Practice makes perfect.'

But Pip had had enough. 'Rubbish, Bruce,' she said brusquely. 'It's all Gemma's doing and you know that. Anything else is just sheer fantasy on your part. Now admit it.'

Bruce mumbled something under his breath but he was not abashed by the ticking off. 'Now this calls for a celebration. I've got a nice surprise organised for you. Dinner at—' he said with a flourish, mentioning a restaurant that was frequented by the rich and famous. What strings had he pulled, Gemma wondered, to get a table reservation at such short notice?

Stefan looked coolly from Gemma to Bruce, his eyes resting on hers hypnotically. 'She'll have to decline your kind invitation, Baxter. Remember part of the prize is dinner with Kevin Ampthill tonight and I believe there he is coming to claim her now. Well done, Gemma.' He nodded at them briefly and

159

touched Gemma on the shoulder as he moved away to mingle with admirers of his popular television programmes which explained the mysteries of the law to the average viewer. It was a spell-binding show, Gemma had often thought, refreshingly direct, ingenious and stylish. Its weekly audience ratings made it one of the most watched peak time shows after some of the well-known soap operas. Kevin Ampthill had detached himself from a group and stood at her elbow. 'The car is at the door Miss Wells so if you'll say goodbye to your friends I'm ready when you are.' He was gorgeous Pip thought, as she watched him smile at Gemma in a way that would have stopped my heart, thought Pip, faintly. Every woman's ideal man. It was a pity he was not Gemma's type, she mused. The girl needed cheering up. If only it had been dinner with Stefan, Gemma thought yearningly. But obviously he did not feel the same way about her. There was a suspicious lump in her throat. There was nothing so miserable as unrequited love she thought despondently. The large limousine belonging to the studio bore them swiftly to the chosen restaurant. The *maître d'hôtel* exchanged a few pleasantries with Kevin Ampthill who seemed to be a regular customer, and showed them to their table, discreetly set apart some distance from others. Waiters moved sure-footed and efficiently. China and silver gleamed on the starched

160

snow-white linen tablecloth.

Gemma had been dreading the ordeal of dinner with Kevin Ampthill. What would she say to him she wondered desperately? The common bond of the competition had been untied and she was sure there was nothing she could find to discuss that could possibly interest him. She did not notice as he assiduously refilled her champagne glass. Soon the nervous tension which had temporarily rendered her silent fell away and she began to come alive again.

'Your presentation to the adjudication panel during the evaluation was so fresh and natural, I wonder if I might be able to interest you in a project that's still on the drawing-board?' he asked casually, as if it was just one of his off-the-cuff remarks. But there was nothing casual in the glance he threw her as he crumbled a bread roll with his fingers. The expression on his face was easy-going but his gaze was shrewd and penetrating. Gemma toyed with the stem of her glass. She could hardly say, 'I'm all ears,' as Pip would have done.

'Tell me about it,' she murmured cautiously. It was the right answer—not too eager or too uninterested.

Kevin Ampthill bent his curly head for a moment and studied her. Then he nodded as if her response met with his professional approval. 'Good. We're planning a series of forty-minute holiday programmes. You know

161

the sort. Reports of holidays actually taken by members of the team. But we want a new member. Someone fresh, responsive—a new face to balance us seasoned professionals. We've held a number of auditions but no one seems to have scored yet. But I think I've found her. It's *you*.'

'Me?' Gemma gasped incredulous. How could she add the spice they were seeking?

He leaned forward, his voice very excited. 'You're just the person holidaymakers will identify with. Natural, fresh, enthusiastic, without being gushing. The true amateur with no axe to grind but to give them what they want. The one truthful voice in the otherwise super packaged, supergloss, grab-your-money-and-run industry. I was very impressed by your showing earlier. You have all the attributes we're looking for—charm, sincerity, looks. You're just right for the job. Now before you say no—' he flashed her that wide disarming smile which millions found irresistible, 'The pay is good.'

Gemma began to protest, but he cut her short gently—again with that smile of his— 'Money *is* everything. Well, it is to me, at any rate! But I'll make it easier for you to say yes. The first pilot programme features a holiday in the Borders—so what could be simpler? You've already done your homework.'

Gemma leaned back in her chair, utterly astounded. 'I don't know what to say,' she

162

managed at last. It was a bolt from the blue. How could he expect her to make a decision just like that?

'I have absolutely no experience of television. I just wouldn't know what to do. I'm a complete ham . . .' her voice tailed off uncertainly.

Kevin Ampthill leaned across, not bothering to conceal his eagerness, and covered her hand with his. 'Don't you see? That's just what we want. The genuine article. Spontaneity. But we'll teach you the basics. All you have to do is be yourself. They'll love that. When I and my producer saw you in action this afternoon, we just couldn't believe our luck. You beat all the other women we'd auditioned, hands down. They were too slick, too hard-boiled, too polished and worst of all too too blasé for the programme we had in mind.'

'And I'm not?' Gemma intervened quickly, not knowing whether to feel pleased or offended. She gave a quick, roguish smile. Kevin Ampthill registered it and was certain that he'd made the right choice. She would give his programme the life and lift-off it needed. He had to persuade her to join it.

And he had to act fast. She was so striking some rival outfit would snap her up.

'Look. Put it this way. Your business is seasonal. You're entering a quiet phase. Sure, you're exploring new ideas, looking to consolidate and expand. But going into Winter

163

you will have more time on your hands. Time when there's no money coming in to the coffers . . .' He raised one fair eyebrow.

Gemma said slowly, 'That's very true.' There was no certainty that she had made the grade with Stefan. But there was one thing of which she was sure. And that was Speedwell's continued existence. It had become an obsession with her. She wanted to see it grow and prosper. She couldn't damp it down just like that. Kevin Ampthill had a point. If the inheritance failed to materialise and no other job prospects presented themselves, she needed a second string to keep the wolf from the door. Whilst all these arguments vied for consideration in her mind, she could not know that he was observing her carefully. At last she reached a decision.

'That's it then. Done and dusted,' he remarked briskly.

She knew why he was so successful. That fatal combination of charm and astuteness was compelling. He handed her his visiting-card. 'Be sure to call me in the morning, otherwise I'll call you!' he said with a touch of irony. 'Then we can fix up a meeting with my producer.' He leaned back in his chair with obvious satisfaction at a hard job, well done.

'He'll be over the moon.' He was referring to his producer. He grinned wickedly, 'Now he owes me a favour.' He said it with obvious relish and Gemma saw that he was completely serious—the sort of man who would extract his price.

Ensuring that she wanted no liqueurs, he signalled to the waiter and signed the bill which, Gemma could see out of the corner of her eye, easily came to three figures.

'Shall we make a move?' He pulled out her chair for her and Gemma preceded him through the crowded restaurant past other diners, conscious of curious eyes on her as they registered her companion.

'Excuse me. Stefan! Good to see you again.' Kevin Ampthill stopped and Gemma paused. He took her elbow. Stefan was dining with a man whose face looked familiar but whom she could not immediately place. 'I am honoured to have had a most charming date tonight with this young lady. The Young Entrepreneur of the Year.'

Stefan stood up, 'Hello again, Gemma.'

Kevin Ampthill looked from one to the other. 'You know each other? How very intriguing.' He was too surprised to be able to conceal it completely.

Stefan interjected smoothly, 'On a professional basis, yes. It could be said we are inextricably bound together.' His eyes never left Gemma's face.

'My you're a dark horse, Gemma!' Kevin Ampthill laughed deep in his throat. 'On trial for your life, eh? Well Stefan's the man to get you acquitted, no doubt about that. And save you for people like me!'

Gemma joined in the laughter, uneasily casting a covert glance in Stefan's direction. His expression was composed, almost blank, but a muscle twitched slightly in his jaw. It was curious, she thought and wondered what it could mean. There followed a brief exchange between the three men which hardly registered with her.

'I will deliver the dear girl safely into the hands of the chauffeur.' She heard the presenter's voice as if through a haze. He had accepted a cigar from Stefan and she realised that he had been invited to join the other two for a post-prandial cognac. He ushered her out to the waiting car. Gemma was relieved. She was exhausted and couldn't have managed another word had he accompanied her home.

'Now don't forget,' Kevin Ampthill reminded her as he poked his head through the rolled down window. 'I'll be waiting for that call of yours.' The chauffeur had collected her case from the hotel and as they pulled up outside her flat she realised with a sense of disbelief that it was 2 a.m. It had been an exciting and momentous day but, despite her exhaustion, she stayed wide awake, her thoughts full of Stefan, until the sun began its journey from the east to put the moon to flight.

CHAPTER SEVEN

Gemma waved until the last of the bikers had swept round the corner. She was strangely reluctant to go back indoors. The place would seem so empty, so dead without them. They were the final party of the season. The grounds of the hotel were ankle deep in Autumn leaves. The weather during the last few weeks had been spectacular. Days of hot, golden sunshine, defying all the forecasts. The motor-cyclists sunbathed on the lawns beneath the red and bronze of the October tints. Winning the Award had made very little difference to this year's bookings but reservations for next year were running at a high level. There had been a run on Speedwell's brochure and it was now reprinting.

'I'll audit your accounts.' The offer from Pip's brother Richard was unexpected and generous. He was now a fully fledged chartered accountant. 'Not as altruistic as it sounds,' he joked, 'You'll be my first own client!' He had offered to do it for next to nothing but despite a friendly argument with Pip, Gemma was adamant. 'No favours, please. You must charge me a proper fee and it must appear in the accounts. It would be distinctly odd if it didn't. Stefan will go over the balance sheet with an eagle eye and I don't want him to think the figures have been enhanced artificially by an accountant's sleight of hand.'

Despite her suspicions that it sounded too good to be true, Kevin Ampthill had lost no time in setting up a meeting for her with his production team. She had wondered, after that wonderful night of surprises, whether he had regretted his decision and would try to wriggle out of it, but he was as good as his word. The contract was signed and soon the episodes would be in rehearsal. Now she had to do some fairly intensive research, seeking out new diversions to interest holidaymakers in the vast and beautiful county of Northumberland. Gemma sat down on the stone bench by the sundial. Everything was going her way. So why should she feel depressed? She knew the answer to that even before she asked it. It was only a matter of days before Richard submitted the Speedwell accounts to Stefan. Then, no doubt, an interminable wait before he delivered his verdict.

'I honestly don't give a damn about the inheritance,' Gemma confessed aloud. And it was true. Regardless of whether the capital was released to her, the only thing that mattered to her was Stefan. Either way there was no avoiding the inevitable—this was the beginning of the end of her involvement with that fascinating, strangely mesmerising man with whom she had fallen head over heels in love. Without him, nothing would be the same, nothing could be the same. She would give almost anything to re-enact the last six months. The struggle to build up Speedwell, even if she had to do it all over again, was nothing compared with the chance to be involved with Stefan again.

'Suppose you had to choose between Stefan and Speedwell?' a nagging little voice drummed in her brain. There was no easy answer to that Gemma pondered. Speedwell was her creation. She had invested more than money in it. Her heart, her mind, her time, her whole being was ineluctably linked to it. But in her heart of hearts, she knew it could never be a substitute for a relationship with Stefan. However satisfying the business, however absorbing it was, when all was said and done Gemma was certain 'beyond all reasonable doubt' not just 'on a balance of probabilities' that if she was compelled to choose between one or the other it would be Stefan Radulescu. But would the choice ever present itself?

As things stood, Gemma had to admit that it looked unlikely. She sighed deeply and stood up, her eyes turning to the indigo sky as if she was seeking some portent. Once indoors, she donned a light multi-coloured woollen jacket over black corduroy trousers. The village hall where the folk music recital was to take place was only five miles away and the Honda bore her there swiftly along poorly lit country roads.

It was ablaze with lights when she arrived and enthusiasts, young and old, thronged its narrow corridors. The local paper had given it a rave write-up and if it was as good as it was rumoured to be, she would find a slot for it on Kevin Ampthill's programme. The tradition of folk music was very strong in these parts and everyone from pit village to farm workers added their voices to the golden old ballads of Northumbria. 'Excuse me,' she smiled apologetically as she edged past knobbly knees to her seat in the second row. The room throbbed with expectation. Conversation turned to applause as a trio of working men came on stage with their home-fashioned musical instruments.

Amidst laughter and snide good-humoured jibes from the audience, they performed their piece.

'Ah but we know who you're really waiting for!' the trio called tantalisingly. Next on the programme was a soloist called Con, who was billed to sing some ballads. She came on quite casually to enthusiastic applause. Gemma did a double take. She was sure she'd seen her before but where? She did a quick mental recall. Then it clicked. It was the girl she'd seen with Stefan in Peggy's. She was a lovely creature, Gemma admitted grudgingly. Her slim frame was clad in tight jeans and she wore a crimson figure hugging pullover patterned with white flowers. Her long, fair hair was tied back in a ponytail. And could she sing! Her accompanist seated himself heavily at a piano in the corner. Soon she had a completely captive audience. Her low, alto voice had an ethereal quality of great sweetness which was utterly enthralling. Her recital was interspersed with her lively comments which had her audience in stitches. The contrast was cleverly planned—a sad lament was followed by a rousing hunting song which prompted the spellbound audience into a paroxysm of whistling and foot stamping.

Gemma joined in. Con was really superb— only twenty yet already so very talented. Gemma felt a pang. But then her reporting instincts took over and she made a firm mental note of everything she had seen and heard. She was sure her producer would be thrilled by this unique display of natural local colour. It was all very informal and relaxed. Halfway through a song people would get up and make for the bar for a drink, weaving their way back to their seats. It was not meant to be disrespectful or offensive. It was just how things were done in these parts. Gemma did likewise cradling the plastic coffee cup in her hands. After the brief interval, which was timed to last fifteen minutes but was nearer thirty, there were a few more acts and then a duo was announced.

Gemma couldn't believe her eyes. By Con's side stood Stefan holding aloft Northumbrian pipes. He had on faded brown trousers, trainers and a heavy knit doe-coloured pullover. He put the pipes to his lips, the girl smiled shyly at him and began to sing. The sound of the pipes filled the room. Gemma leaned forward, her heart beating furiously. He was an accomplished musician—the strange sound of the pipes, plangent, yearning, flowed effortlessly from him. She felt as if her heart would burst in her lungs. Con and Stefan not only performed well together, they looked well together, she thought hollowly. His black hair was a vivid contrast to the pale silk corn of her tresses. There was a sort of rapport between them, a sympathetic blending that transmitted itself to the audience—a sort of symbiosis that seemed to transcend their working relationship. Then the pipes stopped and the song died away. There was thunderous applause. The audience jumped to its feet, cheering and clamouring for an encore.

'More, more,' they demanded. Con tilted her elfin chin at Stefan. He nodded and lifted the pipes to his lips. Gemma realised that she had witnessed a Stefan different from the man she thought she knew. Relaxed, carefree, human. Con must always have seen him like this, known him like this. Gemma felt jealousy knife through her so vehemently she felt as if she was about to be torn apart. Through his love of music, he had revealed to Con much more than he had ever revealed to Gemma, she thought miserably. Con and Stefan—they seemed so close—a unique unit formed by their common interest. Almost mesmerised, she could not take her eyes off Stefan, as during the applause he lightly kissed his partner on the cheek. They stood hand in hand, side by side, smiling and bowing, acknowledging the ovation which seemed never-ending. Con was well known in these parts and a favourite with the audience.

Gemma learned from a crusty-looking man on her right that Stefan had stepped into the breach as a substitute for the piper who generally accompanied her, as he had fallen ill. Afterwards, there was a rush for the bar, Gemma remained seated, collecting her thoughts, her mind a turmoil of conflicting emotions.

'Hello. I spotted you from the stage. Good to see you here.'

Stefan was at the end of the row, his eyes very green. 'Come along and have a drink.'

Gemma forced a bright smile on her lips which felt as if they were frozen together and got up slowly.

'Is there anything wrong?' His voice was very concerned, a thin line between his brows.

'No. Perfect.' With an effort Gemma lightened the tone of her voice, the hard bright smile still on her lips. 'I had no idea you were so accomplished. What other hidden talents do you possess?'

He threw back his head and laughed and stood aside to let her out of the row. 'Nonsense—You're too kind. I'm no match for Con's regular accompanist. You should hear him.'

She noticed how his voice warmed when he uttered Con's name. 'Con's superb,' Gemma remarked mechanically. After all there was little else she could say. It was certainly true and praise for the singer would be expected of her.

'There is something wrong.' Stefan was very still, his eyes probing the mask of her face. 'Can you tell me?' His voice was so sympathetic that she felt like throwing herself into his arms and sobbing her heart out for the man she knew could never be hers.

Gemma gulped, determinedly holding back tears that were so near the surface. 'Nothing organic, I assure you. It's just that the melody and the words are so moving.' The excuse was hastily manufactured—it sounded too glib. Stefan's eyes continued to search her and he was about to say something. Gemma almost wished he would call her bluff in that firm but frank way he had of doing. Instead he said gently, 'That's the magic of the Border ballads and Con knows just how to transmit that magic to the audience. Let's go and find her.'

Gemma could hardly say she'd rather not. It would seem churlish not to want to congratulate the singer and distinctly contradictory if she did not, after all the praise she had heaped on her performance.

Stefan draped an arm round her shoulders and they headed in the direction of the small crowd of well-wishers gathered round the performers. Con broke away and danced up to Stefan, her brown eyes alight. 'We made a good team,' she announced gaily, 'we must do this again.' Gemma murmured her appreciation, feeling utterly excluded as the two good-humouredly teased each other about the wrong notes played and sung. Gemma felt unaccountably weary as if the months of hard toil accumulated in one evening had begun to take its toll. She swayed a little and although Con, busy chattering did not notice it, Stefan was there, an arm unobtrusively under her elbow, pressing her close to him protectively. He registered her face which had gone extremely pale, and began to steer her in the direction of the open door. 'Con, I've some work to catch up on,' he interjected smoothly, still holding Gemma firmly. 'Will you be able to catch a lift home?'

Con nodded vigorously and Gemma saw that she was the sort of girl who would have no shortage of offers. She uttered a mock groan, rolled her eyes and responded in that soft Northumbrian accent, 'Another blood and thunder trial, then? You've an odd way of getting your kicks, Stefan. Bye then.'

Gemma marvelled at her unconcern, her

total insouciance about what she Gemma would have regarded as a sudden and early departure from the rest of the roisterers.

'I'll see you anon,' Stefan grinned at Con's back already fast retreating into a huddle of admirers.

Once out into the fresh moonlit night, he took command. 'Right, now you're going straight to bed, my darling Gemma. You look dead beat.'

'That's the price of success,' Gemma managed a weak smile.

'Rubbish,' he countered firmly, 'That's a recipe for disaster. You must do something about having a holiday now everything's over.'

'I didn't think holidays featured in your scheme of things for me,' she said faintly.

He gave a snort. 'Your general perception of me as an overbearing trustee or some sort of Simon Legree is interesting, if way off the mark. Anyone would think from the way you talked that I was totally antipathetic towards you whereas . . .' his voice tailed off. His eyes met hers but Gemma, immersed in her own misery, could learn nothing from his steady gaze. Unexpectedly he rubbed a finger along her cheek and the gentle gesture was so overwhelming in its comfort, she could control her emotions no longer. Tears rolled down her face. She was too depressed, too weary of the battle to care anymore. 'Hush Gemma. Come on. I'll take you back to the hotel.'

176

'You can't,' Gemma sniffed as her sobs began to subside. 'I've got my bike with me.'

'Oh damn the bike,' he said dismissively, 'It's not coming with us this time. Leave it locked up here. I'll send someone over to collect it for you in the morning.' He hurried her to the XJ6 and they drove the short distance back to the hotel in silence. Glancing at his profile from time to time only made her feel much worse, only too conscious as she was that there was only a slim chance to be with him, beside him, like this again before they parted company for good. No more would she see those strong hands on the wheel, that strong profile lit by the moon, that deep, seductive voice that made her shiver with pleasure. But Speedwell would go on. Born of her unexpected link with Stefan, it was destined to outlive her present links with him. The irony of it all was too devastating to contemplate. She couldn't go on with Speedwell she felt, suddenly. She had proved she could do it and do it well. It would need her continuous effort and unflagging patience and presence. All she wanted to do now was to get as far away from it as possible and forget it, for it was an unceasing reminder of Stefan.

'Here you are, delivered safe and sound.' He drew up outside the front entrance and sprang round to open the door for her. He kissed her on the cheek, 'Goodnight Gemma. Have a good night's sleep and think seriously about that holiday in the morning, promise? Oh, by the way, your accountant has sent me your company's accounts. They arrived through the post today . . .' He paused and looked at her keenly. 'I'm analysing them and unless some crisis blows up in chambers, you'll be hearing from me shortly.'

Gemma thanked him politely for the lift and fled indoors only too aware of those searching eyes. There was nothing to keep her here in the Borders. Her research for the holiday programme was complete and Speedwell's season had come to an end.

The next morning, Gemma came downstairs, her suitcase packed. 'Miss Wells— your bike is round the back. Lloyd from the garage brought it over twenty minutes ago,' the receptionist said.

So Stefan had not forgotten the bike. There were goodbyes all round as she shook hands with the hotel staff, promising to see them all again the following year. Stefan had had the Honda spruced up for her, and his thoughtfulness brought a lump to her throat. The bike shone under the Autumn sunlight. A couple of kick starts and she was away. At the railway station, she hoisted it into the guard's van and the train bore her swiftly down to King's Cross Station.

*   *   *

'How are you going to pass the time, until you hear from Stefan?' Pip asked cautiously. 'Remember how he kept you in suspense after your uncle's death?'

'Don't remind me about that,' Gemma said with a shudder. 'If this is going to be like an action replay, I'll have to take a long trip away from it all.'

She sighed. To be honest, she didn't feel inclined to leave her Blackheath flat just then. After months of living like an exile in one room, it was wonderful to be back and to have the whole place to herself. But if she'd didn't go on holiday, she'd only brood about the outcome. And if she did go away, she might miss Stefan's summons. It was a classic Catch 22 situation.

Pip sensed her dilemma. 'When in doubt, don't,' she suggested wisely.

Gemma nodded. Her friend's advice matched what she had virtually decided for herself.

The two of them had reached the cinema where a highly acclaimed comedy film was showing. It was what they both needed and they stumbled out afterwards shaking with laughter.

'It was hilarious,' choked Gemma as she rode pillion behind Pip.

'Didn't that chap remind you of Bruce?' Pip called over her shoulder as she stopped at a red traffic light.

Gemma had not given Bruce a moment's thought for a long time. 'What's he up to these days?'

Pip shook her head, 'Dunno. Richard mentioned to me that Bruce had tried to contact him several times in succession recently but Richard has been too busy with clients' audits to meet up with him. Richard reckons he's into some all consuming get-rich-quick scheme from the sounds of it and Richard is so intrigued he told me that when time allows, he'll quiz him about it. I expect Bruce will surface sooner or later and then you won't be able to fight him off.'

The lights changed and Gemma was saved the embarrassment of thinking up a convincing response. Back at the flat, Gemma made up her mind to tackle her friend. 'You know Bruce was always hinting at wanting me to hand over my money for him to invest. Did he know about the inheritance?' She looked Pip straight in the eye.

Pip didn't bat an eyelid. 'If you mean, did I say anything to him about it, then the answer's no.' She didn't seem at all offended by the question. Gemma was relieved. Her friendship with Pip was firm and of long standing, but she had to be sure. 'But I mentioned it to my brother, I confess, although he promised to keep it confidential. Maybe, he unwittingly let slip something to Bruce who hoped to make the most of it. You know, something in the

180

course of party gossip.'

'Anyway,' Gemma lifted up the wings of the bottle opener and uncorked the red wine, 'it's not mine yet and might well never be.'

Pip blinked disbelievingly. 'Surely not! Speedwell is a resounding success through your own efforts. Nobody could have done any better. It's brilliant. Stefan is either a lunatic or grossly unjust if he thinks otherwise.' Her face went red with anger. 'And if he doesn't make it over to you,' she clenched her fists. 'I'll . . . I'll . . . sue him for it.'

Gemma laughed at her champion. Pip could always be relied on to take up the cudgels on behalf of a worthy cause. 'Just you say when you want me to issue the writ!'

Gemma said idly, 'Do you mind if I switch on the tv.? I know it's antisocial but the engineer came to fix it this morning and I haven't had a chance to test his handiwork, yet.'

Pip yawned, her mind still on the film they'd just seen. 'Go ahead, don't mind me.' She stretched out her legs and sipped the warming wine.

Gemma turned on the television news. Bruce's face was briefly pictured on the screen as the newscaster finished a news item ' . . . Baxter arrested for insider dealings is seen here arriving at Bishopsgate Police Station with C.I.D. officers . . .'

'Oh my God . . .' whispered Pip, her face

suddenly pallid with horror. They exchanged appalled glances, momentarily at a loss for words. Arrested like a common criminal, the brief television sighting of Bruce showed him unemotional, poker-faced as he was hustled, flanked by detectives, into the station from a police car.

'How can we help?' Pip asked. They both knew it was an unanswerable question. Knowing Bruce, he must have hired the best defence lawyers money could buy. Gemma shook her head, almost automatically. The news made her feel stunned, cold. They both knew that Bruce was a smooth operator. That was his persona, it was part of his job. But this . . . this was quite different. This was a nasty crime, using inside knowledge of a company's affairs in order to make a profit for oneself at the expense of legitimate dealers. Personal gain—it was tainted money.

'Did you hear what the newscaster said, "Other arrests are expected shortly".' Pip buried her head in her hands. 'I just have to scoot. I've got to know if Richard's implicated in any way in this mess. But I want to phone him first.' She sprang to the telephone and keyed in his number. Gemma slipped tactfully out of the room ostensibly to brew some coffee. She could hear Pip shrilly interrogating her brother. After what she calculated was a decent interval, Gemma returned to the sitting-room.

182

Pip looked as if she had been put out of her misery, her anguished expression replaced by one of relief. 'Glory be. Saved by a whisker. Richard had to cancel dinner with Bruce a few weeks ago owing to toothache. He'd kicked himself for it. Bruce had been pretty mysterious about it all, saying that he had certain information which would make them both a fortune, but Bruce wouldn't say any more over the phone.'

'But surely Richard would have realised it was illegal?' Gemma protested, scandalised.

Pip nodded, 'Oh I'm sure Richard wouldn't have used it. But you know, guilt by association and all that. The fact that he'd known about it would have made him suspect. Anyway Richard's assured me that the limit of his involvement with Bruce has been that of socialising, nothing more. Gosh, what a narrow escape,' she giggled suddenly. 'Richard was rather indignant really. Said I didn't have much faith in his judgement of Bruce as a person who sailed close to the wind.'

Gemma smiled, sharing to her friend's sense of deliverance. 'Poor Bruce,' she murmured, sympathy welling up in her despite the fact that he had only himself to blame.

Pip, now that her brother was well and truly exonerated, was not so charitable. 'Serves him right,' she snorted, self-righteously. She tossed her head, 'Richard said he knew he'd come a cropper, sooner or later. I think he's despicable, taking undue advantage of inside knowledge like that.'

She stood up and brushed a few crisps crumbs from her trousers. Gemma could see that she couldn't wait to get the low-down from her brother, and she saw her to the door. Well, Pip was one visitor Bruce need not count on in his lonely prison cell, she thought wryly. Gemma wandered back into her sitting-room and poured herself another glass of wine. Her thoughts turned to Stefan. By now he was bound to have heard that Bruce was in the hot seat, she imagined. It would be interesting to learn what he made of it. But then she didn't expect she would ever know. The likelihood of that filled her with a sense of deep depression. She had to stop thinking about him like this, or she would make herself ill, she told herself firmly.

Next morning every paper shrieked the news of Bruce's arrest. They hinted that further revelations would soon enfold. Speculation on the amount that he was alleged to have made from his insider trading was rife and ranged from anything between four and seven figures. There were highly coloured accounts of his executive life-style, his expensive tastes and his penchant for pretty girls. The one thing that united the editors was their unanimous condemnation of 'this vile white collar crime'. 'City hangs its head in shame' screamed one headline.

The media kept up their relentless denunciation of what was being described as 'Scandal City', and the following week there were graphic accounts of Bruce's first appearance at the magistrates' court. His lawyer applied for bail but it was vigorously opposed by counsel for the prosecution, the eminent QC Stefan Radulescu. Gemma gasped. The Crown was certainly rolling out its big guns for the event. Stefan's fee would be astronomical. According to the crime correspondent's report, Stefan had objected to bail on the grounds that the defendant Bruce would undoubtedly attempt to flee from London to find refuge abroad—somewhere like Latin America, in a steamy country there with which Britain had no extradition treaty.

But despite a desperate counter-argument from Bruce's counsel that his client was willing to surrender his passport to the police, the plea was rejected. He was remanded in custody and marched down to the cells to await a further hearing at a later date. So Stefan was prosecuting Bruce! Gemma read the item with mixed emotions. Dismay was uppermost. From the little she knew of such trials, it was likely to be long and complicated. A dedicated barrister like Stefan would set aside all other peripheral matters including his assessment of Speedwell, until justice had been done. Gemma bit her lip; it was ironic that yet again Bruce was responsible for wreaking havoc in her life. How could she possibly live in suspended animation? But it seemed to her she had no alternative. To approach Stefan now to persuade him to make an early decision about Speedwell could well be counter-productive. He would accuse her of being self-seeking, demanding and grasping. Couldn't she see that he had more pressing things to do in the public interest? So real did the remonstrating words sound in her ear that at first she did not hear the telephone ring. It rang again with that shrill persistence that telephones possess.

It was a voice which took her some moments to recognise, so many months having passed since she had last heard it. 'Mr Radulescu wishes you to attend at his flat in Eaton Square tomorrow evening in connection with the administration of your late uncle's estate,' Stefan's clerk informed her pompously. 'I believe you know the address, but in case you have mislaid it . . .'

Gemma let him intone, her thoughts awhirl. It was a bombshell and its sheer unexpectedness startled her and made her feel uneasy. Stefan must want to get it over with— to release her from all the guesswork so that she could make positive decisions about her future. 'Please let him know I'll be there,' she said, forgetting to ask when he expected her to arrive.

'He will see you at seven-thirty Miss Wells.'

There was a sharp click as he crisply replaced the receiver.

*   *   *

It was early November and people were beginning to sport Remembrance Day poppies. Gemma woke to a day of thick mist and the beginnings of what looked like being a very cold snap. Frost sparkled on the short winter grass of the heath. All morning a sense of tension enveloped her which clung to her even after she had thoroughly serviced and polished her bike, an activity which could usually be guaranteed to blow away the blues. The thick mist did not lift and on the radio she heard reports of pile-ups in fog. Deciding it would be safer in present conditions if she left the bike behind, she caught a bus up to Central London. She had dressed carefully; over a brushed cotton shirt she donned a charcoal, wide-trousered flannel trouser suit with a short peplum waisted jacket. An Italian felt hat and leather gauntlets completed the stylish effect. As a morale booster she inserted *diamanté* dove-shaped ear-rings.

Gemma took infinite trouble with her make-up, carefully outlining her mouth with Estée Lauder woodland rose lipstick. Lightly she stroked brandy/cinnamon eyeshadow on her eyelids and added the finishing touch to her eyelashes with luscious mascara. Her hair

187

was brushed loosely to her shoulders. She stared critically at her face and immediately felt much better. There was nothing like some expensive cosmetics to give one Dutch courage, she owned.

Promptly at the appointed hour, Gemma rang the doorbell of Stefan's apartment building; his buzzer went immediately. The lift swept her swiftly and silently to his top-floor penthouse with its stunning views across London's most prestigious square. He was standing at the open door of his flat, waiting for her. His face looked drawn and grey as if he was badly in need of a long carefree holiday, she thought with a pang. He was formally dressed in a classically elegant pure wool Prince of Wales check double-breasted suit, a cotton pin-stripe shirt and a restrained, dark blue silk tie. His black leather shoes were unmistakably hand-made.

'Not sherry, of course,' he teased, pouring out vodka and tonic from an array of bottles on a walnut console table.

'You remembered!' exclaimed Gemma, taking the glass from him.

'How could I forget?' he returned with a smile. He did not pour out a drink for himself which was surely significant, she decided. It could mean that he was impatient to keep another appointment and was unwilling to linger over the business in hand. That seemed ominous. The meeting was obviously intended to be short and sharp. She braced herself and took a nervous sip before asking quickly.

'Why shouldn't you forget?' It sounded more truculent than she had meant but she did not apologise. Anyone in her position was entitled to show some emotion.

For a moment he seemed taken aback at her ungracious tone. 'You do, of course, know why I invited you to come here this evening?'

Gemma nodded, her nerves temporarily depriving her of speech, and laid down the crystal glass carefully on the pickled-pine coffee table. Her lips felt dry and she cleared her throat.

Stefan turned and flipped open the antique roll-top desk behind him. He withdrew a slim package tied round with lawyers' pink tape and handed it to her.

Gemma stared down at it. 'What is this?' she flashed him an anxious glance, her face pale with apprehension.

'I think you ought to see for yourself,' he suggested softly.

Gemma undid the tape with trembling fingers and pulled out the document. It was in black type on thick, creamy paper.

'Won't you read it aloud to me?' His voice was very gentle. As if in a dream she did as he bade her—

' " . . . This Assent . . ." ' she began falteringly, and then gaining in confidence continued ' " . . . Stefan Radulescu as Personal

189

Representative of the said Arthur Wells hereby assents to the vesting in Gemma Elizabeth Wells of all that piece or parcel of land together with the building and appurtenances erected thereon or on some part thereof situate at . . ."' It set out in full the address of her late uncle's house in Northumberland. '". . . to hold unto the Beneficiary in fee simple".'

The legal jargon meant nothing to her and she gazed at him puzzled and uncertain.

'You're holding the title deeds to Arthur's house which I, as the administrator of his estate, have formally signed over to you. You own it now. It's all yours, as is the rest of the inheritance which, as you know, is considerable. You passed his test with flying colours, Gemma. I'm *so* glad. What do you think you'll do now?'

Gemma was stunned, feeling quite unable to react. She said nothing but studied the contents of the Assent over and over again until she almost knew it by heart. It was unbelievable. She had always thought that no matter how well she did, Stefan would say it was not good enough and find some convincing reason for withholding, if not the whole inheritance then at least a sizeable part of it. She had begun to believe that he did not approve of women of her age coming into a fortune.

'I don't know what to say,' she murmured, at

last. It dawned on her that she need never work again.

'Well, this will loosen your tongue,' Stefan said mischievously as he poured her another drink. This time he mixed one for himself and raised his glass to her.

'Congratulations. It was well deserved. Arthur would have been so proud of you. But I'm sure he can see you now, up there twanging his harp, rubbing his hands with glee and relishing this moment.'

'To Uncle Arthur who had the last word.' Gemma toasted her canny relative.

Stefan said quietly, 'I expect at a time like this, it's all tinged with a certain sadness.' He reached out and touched her hand. 'Baxter's arrest for insider dealing must have left you utterly shaken.' He grimaced. 'I'm sorry I can't be more reassuring or helpful for obvious reasons as I'm the chief prosecutor. But believe me Gemma, I'd do anything for your happiness.'

Gemma rose to her feet and crossed to the window, looking down into the King's Road which ran alongside the square. The passing cars looked like dinky toys. 'It was a shock, admittedly. He is, was, I know, inclined to be a bit casual about things. I am sorry for him, just as I would feel sorry for anyone in the same position, but no more than that. I'm hardly likely to take up my loom while I wait for him to serve his sentence.'

Stefan stared at her. 'What do you mean? What are you saying?' he questioned. 'Are you telling me that Baxter was no more to you than a casual acquaintance?'

She could hear his breathing quickening.

Gemma returned to the stylish pale blue leather armchair and crossed her legs. Stefan seemed intense and very vulnerable.

'Of course. I thought you knew that.' She wanted to add, 'He could never be more than that to me so long as you were around.'

Stefan bent over her, his face very close to hers. 'I must know for certain,' he persisted, a strangely urgent tone to his voice.

Gemma sensed the gravity of the moment. At any other time she might have made a flippant throwaway remark but somehow tonight was different. She gazed at him steadily with wide blue eyes, her lips only inches away from his.

'Bruce may have thought he was making progress with me but as far as I was concerned it was platonic. Oh yes, I don't deny it. I was very lonely in my bid to make a success of Speedwell and so anxious to prove to you that I could make it—not just for the sake of the inheritance but also because . . . because I desperately wanted your approval. Bruce just happened to be there initially with a muddled sort of support, in the right place at the right time, to use the cliché . . . !'

'And . . .' Stefan's eyes on her face were

warm and gentle.

'But how could I take someone like Bruce seriously after all his antics? He could have ruined Speedwell if I'd let him.'

'So there is nothing between you and Baxter. Is that what you're trying to say?'

'That's what I am saying,' Gemma insisted softly. 'Bruce made me realise who I wanted and needed—only you.'

Stefan reached out and took both her hands in his. 'Dearest, darling Gemma. That is the best present you could ever give me. And all the time I was convinced you were in love with Baxter. I felt so wretched—you seemed so remote, so far from me, so wrapped up in him.'

Gemma pressed his hand to her breast and held it there.

'And all the time I was so sure you didn't care for me—that you were only concerned to be rid of me and that encumbering trusteeship as soon as decently possible.'

He framed her face in his hands, his lips meeting hers. 'I have loved you from the moment we were ill met in the storm,' he confessed. He took her hand in his and guided her across the room to the sofa. 'I want you to sit beside me here, so that I can feel you are near me and real and not just a dream. I couldn't bear it if you left me again. When you sped away from me after that night in the barn I could have kicked myself that I'd let you go without getting your address. I was so

193

desperate to see you again that I was about to hire a private eye and pay just about anything he wanted to track you down. Then when I discovered in my chambers that day that I'd been appointed your trustee, I couldn't believe my luck. Fate had delivered you into my orbit again. But, believe me, it was sheer hell seeing you trying to fulfil Arthur's conditions—seeing you having to cope with all the ups and downs. If I seemed somewhat short at times it was only because I so desperately wanted to help you but knew I must not. That I had to keep myself at arm's length. But, if only you knew how tempted I was to abort Arthur's challenge.' He kissed her as any lover might kiss his girl after a long absence.

Gemma gave a deep long sigh and stroked his forehead, 'And so you decided to take your time,' she reproved him gently, 'And now may I ask about Con?'

Stefan's head jerked up, his eyes brooding. 'Con? What about her?' He saw the pained expression in Gemma's lifted eyes and relented.

'Darling. She's a super lassie but there's nothing between us save . . .' he gave her a crooked, wicked smile and then kissed her again. '. . . Pavel and Marianne's son. He's her fiancé. They're getting married soon as we will, I hope.' His fingers stroked her cheek and his arm around her tightened.

'Very soon,' Gemma murmured drowsily.

194

Stefan kissed her again fiercely and she kissed him back, their hearts beating together. All the misunderstanding, misery and wretchedness of the past few weeks melted away and she had found peace at last. 'Arthur was right,' he mused.

'So you keep saying—in more ways than one. But which one in particular?'

'You'll like my niece Gemma, he told me. One day lad, you'll get to meet and know her.' Gemma could almost hear her uncle's booming Northumbrian tones. 'She's the right lass for you.'

'And am I?' Gemma couldn't resist the query. There was a sub text of insecurity behind her seemingly teasing remark.

'Well, you're not for Bruce,' Stefan said very firmly, his expression suddenly very taut and intense. He drew her to him again and they leaned against each other. 'And you'll always be mine.'

'Poor Bruce,' Gemma reflected, her eyes closed. Stefan snorted.

'Don't waste another moment's sympathy on him. He deliberately misused confidential information for his own greedy ends.'

'Then you've found him guilty even before his trial has begun,' Gemma protested passionately.

Stefan shut his eyes as if it was a painful subject he preferred not to talk about. He pressed a finger to her lips.

'I am not prejudging him,' he said patiently, shaking his head. 'That's for the judge and jury.'

Gemma wound her arms round him. 'You always have an answer to everything. You're a clever, clever man and I love you in spite of that. But I can't believe this is happening to me,' she said dreamily.

Stefan's face relaxed and he claimed her lips with his own in a long and tender kiss.

'Neither can I,' Stefan admitted when he released her. He gave her a loving glance, 'But it is. And it will keep on happening, Gemma I promise you.' He delved into his pocket and withdrew a large solitaire diamond ring mounted in platinum. 'You're the best thing that's happened to me. I adore you.' He slipped it on her finger. 'Now you're *my* fiancée and nothing can keep us apart. I want to spend the rest of my life with you, my sweetheart.'

His words were those she'd longed to hear for so long, she thought joyfully.

He gave a contented sigh as he held her close in his arms and seeing the depth of love in his eyes, Gemma's happiness was complete.